THE KILLER'S WIFE

Also by Susan Furlong

What They Don't Know
Shattered Justice
Fractured Truth
Splintered Silence
War and Peach
Rest in Peach
Peaches and Scream

Written as Lucy Arlington

Off the Books
Played by the Book

THE KILLER'S WIFE

SUSAN FURLONG

SEVENTH STREET BOOKS®

Published 2023 by Seventh Street Books®

Cover images © Shutterstock
Cover design by Jennifer Do
Cover design © Start Science Fiction

Inquiries should be addressed to
Start Science Fiction
221 River Street, 9th Floor
Hoboken, NJ 07030

Phone: 212-431-5455
www.seventhstreetbooks.com

10 9 8 7 6 5 4 3 2 1

ISBN: 978-1-64506-057-4 (paperback)
ISBN: 978-1-64506-073-4 (ebook)

Printed in the United States of America

Patrick:
You would've loved this one.

The worst prison would be a closed heart.

—*Saint John Paul II*

Strange Murders: *"The Hatchet Killer"*
Transcript of the original episode, four years ago

Host Wesley Steele: Tonight's episode brings you the story of the unsolved murders of three young women, their bodies brutally dismembered and their suspected killer, Lucas Yates, missing. We have reconstructed the events of this story in precise detail in hopes that someone, somewhere knows the truth. Whenever possible, the actual community members and police officials involved in this case have participated in recreating these events. Join me for this episode of Strange Murders ; the key to this crime could be in your hands.

PROLOGUE

He stands with his back against the old hickory, staring at her window lit up like a gleaming spotlight on the dark stage of night. Her face is lifted to the stars, away from the murky shadows of tree-filled hills. Away from him.

Every nerve in his body is stretched like a taut wire as he watches her. *Is it good, Kerry, to finally see the world outside of gray prison walls?* Four years is a long time. Too long. Women harden in prison, there is no avoiding it. Her body is no longer round and soft, but a series of sharp lines and stringy muscles, her hair a mop of black razored edges like an anime drawing. Maybe someone should erase her and start again.

She steps back into the room, and he's left alone in the dark, nothing but the clicking of tree frogs and buzzing of mosquitos. *Come back,* he longs to call out. He sighs and pulls out a piece of crinkled newsletter from The Hatchet Club that he'd found discarded. In the dark, he can't make out the words, not that he needs to. He's read it several times. But with Kerry back now, in her grandfather's cabin only a few yards from him, he can't resist reading it again. His pulse quickens as he pulls out his penlight and flicks it over the words: *Reliable sources confirm that the killer's wife, Kerry Grey, is returning to Joy to serve two years of parole, leaving members to wonder if her presence will draw Lucas from the depths of the Kootenai. Or does she already know where he's hiding?*

THE KILLER'S WIFE

He shakes his head, *Kerry, Kerry, Kerry*. The wife of an accused serial killer, your story aired on *Strange Murders* to millions of viewers. How messed up is that? And poor Joey, what must it be like to be the young son of The Hatchet Killer?

He crumples the sheet in his hand and catches a movement at the window. She's now pressed against the glass, looking his way. His breath catches, as if she can see him, as if she might come to him, tell him—

Suddenly she snatches the curtain and pulls it tight.

He kills the penlight and steps back into the trees.

~ PART I ~
THE RETURN

Strange Murders: *"The Hatchet Killer"*
Transcript of the original episode, four years ago

Host Wesley Steele: Joy, Montana, a sleepy mountain town with scenic views, quaint shops and lively bars, seemed like the perfect place to either take a break and cut loose before college classes started or to celebrate after the rigors of college. During the summer of 2014, three women, unknown to each other, two who were recent high school graduates and another who had just finished her nursing degree came to Joy to do just that. Samantha Brodie, Emily Lynn, and Abby Marshal traveled here from different parts of the country to hike the trails, swim in the glacier-fed lakes, and take part in the local party scene. But each mysteriously disappeared. And unfortunately, what should have been a normal rite of passage became a bloodbath of terror for these three innocent young women.

ONE

Adam Nash

It's Monday morning and still dark outside when I slip from bed and creep away from my sleeping wife to hide in the attic and watch, for the umpteenth time, my favorite episode of *Strange Murders*.

Lucas Yates, "the Hatchet Killer." Three bloody murders, all in one summer. The year was 2014, and back then the story was a blip on my radar, news lost amid bigger headlines: ISIS, Robin Williams's suicide, the Ebola outbreak . . . a dreary year in the news, but I paid little attention to any of it. At twenty-two, I lived a self-absorbed life thousands of miles away in Chicago, on break from my college classes, partying, and hanging with Miranda, my then girlfriend, now wife. What did Lucas Yates and the women he murdered in Joy, Montana, have to do with me?

Nothing. Until the story became an episode on *Strange Murders*.

A remnant of my childhood when I was weaned on episodes of true crime television, seated on the sofa next to Mother while ash dwindled on cigarette after cigarette, her eyeballs bulging and lower lip gnawed raw as she ferreted clues from the show, and then squawked, "Adam!" "Get me that phone and punch in 1-800-CrimeTV. I need to tell those idiots a thing or two about investigating crime."

Her claim to her authority resulted from the day she called in a tip that led to the capture of Wayne Cox, wanted for the murder of two store clerks in Skokie. She'd recognized his profile in line at the local Gas Mart—"I'd know that birthmark anywhere"—and when he left, she'd followed him to the parking lot of a cheap motel down the street and called the cops. Turns out, she was right. He was holed up there, hidden in plain sight.

The story exploded in the news: *Local Woman Helps Bring Killer to Justice.* Reporters came to the house to interview Mother. I warm at the memory of the frenzy of activity, photos, and questions, and the man from the local news channel with a mic in his hand. We recorded the news that night on our VCR, and in the days that followed, I replayed the tape over and over, rewatching the part where Mama mentioned me on camera. "My little armchair detective," she called me, like we were a team, like I'd helped somehow, and I was hooked. Obsessed, more like it. Mother never had much gumption, not enough to abuse me, nor enough to neglect me; we simply existed together, two bumps on the sofa, until that single moment when she'd coupled us in that public glory, sparking our relationship, the flame growing until a burning desire to please her raged inside me. Anything to recapture that fleeting gleam of pride in her eye. It's the reason I became a cop. And the reason I eventually left the force, but that's another story. Not a happy one, either. But in the end, when the cancer had about eaten up both of my mother's lungs, I spent as much time as I could with her, watching another one of our favorite shows, *Strange Murders.*

"The Hatchet Killer" was the final episode we saw together. I'll never forget what she said that evening as she coughed and wheezed, every breath an effort: "Oh, Adam, what I wouldn't give for us to be the ones to find that damn killer."

She died the next day. Since then, I've spent my free time collecting information on the case. Just like this most current news article I found on a late-night internet dive into the life of Lucas Yates. A tabloid piece about his wife, Kerry, written to generate clicks as it ruins lives. Trash reporting, and I feel slimy reading it, let alone printing it so I can reread it later, but finding Lucas Yates was Mama's dying wish. And now it's part of my new job.

Weird News Online
Your Source for Strange Stories

Wife of Notorious Serial Killer Left Holding the Bag
Accused Montana serial killer Lucas Yates is suspected of murdering at least three women during the summer of 2014, dismantling their corpses with a hatchet, and spreading their body parts across the Kootenai Forest. But before he was dubbed the Hatchet Killer, he was thought to be just a normal hard-working husband and father, married to Kerry Yates, a young waitress in Joy, Montana. Although Kerry claims she had no idea of her husband's penchant for murder, the severed finger of his third victim was found inside a shopping bag in the back seat of her vehicle. With Lucas long-gone, Mrs. Yates was left holding the bag with this damning evidence, yet she still maintained her ignorance and her husband's innocence. The court of law, however, sentenced her to six years for felony Accessory After the Fact. In a cruel twist of fate, Mrs. Yates is currently serving prison time, while her notorious husband has disappeared. He sure gave his wife "the finger" . . . in more ways than one.

Six years in Montana Woman's Prison (MWP), four years served, and now for two years she'll be on parole.

And I'm to be her parole officer.

I fold the paper, cram it into my pocket, and feel a pulse of anticipation. The thought of meeting Kerry gives me a rush like I haven't felt for years. Something intensely cerebral yet primal. I can't wait to get inside her head, pick apart her brain, see what makes her tick. *How could you* not *know your husband was a monster, Kerry? Did you watch as he hacked away at their bodies? Did you help?*

Strange Murders: *"The Hatchet Killer"*
Transcript of the original episode, four years ago

Interview with Kerry Grey's former classmate: Kerry was always different, even back in grade school. I remember one time she came to school with a brown paper bag, and inside it was a skull of some sort of animal. She was proud of killing it with her own hands. Said she'd shot it with a rifle or shotgun or something. She was big into hunting and fishing, all that stuff. I think they lived in the mountains somewhere, preppers maybe. You know the type? She didn't really fit in with the other kids at school, but I don't think she cared. She was a loner.

TWO

Kerry Grey

Coffee is still warm in the pot, so I pour two mugs, in case Pops wants another, and meet him outside by the creek. His shirt is off, and it's the first time I notice just how much his bulky frame has diminished these past four years. He's leaner, more angular. Still, at seventy, his arms move with sinewy precision as he hurls the blade into the wood . . . *thwack, thud, thwack, thud* . . . He sees me, stops, and flings the blade at the stump, burying the wedge to the haft.

"Thank you." He reaches for the mug. "Just what I need. Got about a half cord of wood that needs splitting and bundling this morning."

I nod and my gaze follows Boone, our dog, as he wanders over the gentle slope of our land, past Joey's treehouse and the small barn for Pop's woodworking, through a clump of blossoming fruit trees, and to the chicken house where he sniffs the perimeter. Beyond our land, the trees of the Kootenai line up like thousands of dark arrows piercing the sky. The quietness here is deafening. I rub my shoulders, roll my neck, and breathe in thin, pine-scented air, willing my nerves to calm. That spark of light I saw last night—

"Kerry?"

I blink. "Yeah?"

"I was asking how you slept."

"Okay, I guess." I look away again, shrug.

"I'm glad you're home." His voice is gentle. Quiet. The little girl in me wants to be engulfed in his arms, warm and safe. Instead, I say, "I'm only staying until I'm off parole. You know that, right? Everyone knows me here. It's that damn show, everyone's seen it. It's too hard on Joey to have people talking about us all the time. I'm going to save some money and take him somewhere and start over again."

"Forget about that show. Forget about other people. You know the truth. That's all that matters."

"Yeah, but Joey."

"What about him?"

"His dad's a deranged serial killer. All his friends know it, and everyone believes it except him. How many times has he said that his dad's no killer? A lot, just since I've been home. Bet that's what he says all the time. He does, doesn't he? He can't accept that his father killed those women."

"I've heard it. School counselor says that he knows it's the truth, but he's not ready to admit it yet. She says not to push him."

"School counselor?"

"Yeah. He sees her once a week."

"Once a week? I didn't know that."

"Because I haven't told you yet. It's a new thing. Look, you just got back. Don't try to take on everything right away."

A faint *chuff-chuff-chuff* of helicopter blades beats the air, and Pops shields his eyes, squinting into the sky. "Lost hiker. Heard about it this morning on the radio." He sips his coffee and we both stare at the woods quietly, looking anywhere except at one another. How did we get this way, Pops and me? Talking seemed easier before, behind plexiglass.

"I saw a light at the edge of the woods last night," I finally say.

"Light?" He turns to me.

"Something small, glowing. Just for a second, then it was gone."

"A trick of moonlight glinting off animal's eyes likely. You've been locked up so long you forgot what night's like on the mountain."

"Maybe." I suck in a ragged breath. There's a cliff of fear I dangle over every time there is a news story about a woman gone missing, or a runaway girl. "They say he's still out there. Some folks think they've spotted him. Others say it's his ghost haunting the woods. And there's this club in town—"

"Don't pay attention to none of that. Stories, that's all those are. It's been over four years. Even if Lucas is still alive, he's not coming back. Don't you worry, honey."

"Yeah, but if he does?"

His jaw tightens. "He's not coming back. I know this isn't easy, what with parole and being back here in Joy, all of this with Joey, but you got to stay positive. Look at the good things: you're home, you got your son . . ."

"And you."

"And me." He smiles, and his smile pulls me back from that cliff. "Don't get tripped up by your past. Thank the good Lord for what you have and look at this like the first day of the rest of your life. Okay?"

I mull that over. "The first day of the rest of my life."

"That's right. And you can start by getting Joey off to school." He sets his coffee mug aside and picks up the splitter again. The conversation is over.

I toss the rest of my coffee into the weeds and take one final glance at the surrounding woods. I can't shake the feeling that Lucas is still out there, lurking somewhere in the darkness of the Kootenai, watching me.

* * *

The ride to school was quiet. I tried, but Joey responded to my questions with barely more than a grunt, then asked to be dropped a block from the school. Now, as I push my way through the hall, I'm surrounded by students shouting, laughing, swearing even, intercoms buzzing, chairs scraping, lockers clinking, all cloaked in the smell of sweat, disinfectant, and bubblegum lip gloss. Suddenly, I'm seven again, back in Mrs. Sills's second-grade room. It's show and tell time, and I'm cross-legged on a colorful rug with a crumpled paper bag in front of me as I patiently wait my turn. I'm small and knobby with brown tangled hair and eyes too big for my face, and I always smell of woodsmoke and wind and stand out in my feed-store jeans and flannel shirts, but today I have something special to show. Something that will make the other kids like me better.

Finally, Mrs. Sills points to me, and I yank it from the bag, flashing it around the circle of scrunched faces: a skull with antlers. A small buck and my first shotgun kill.

All smiles, I ask, "Isn't he a beauty? Killed 'im myself. Pops helped me skin and boil the head."

One girl's eyes, rounded with terror, flit between me and my prized trophy as she points and shrieks, "Killer Kerry."

Soon the others join in until the whole room fills with chanting: *Killer Kerry, Killer Kerry.*

My new nickname.

It stuck and came back to haunt me years later over what others figured to be a much smaller souvenir—a finger. Still haunts me today: both the name and the finger.

A shiver threatens. Some claim that I've lived up to my childhood nickname. Even now, as kids look my way, bending their heads and whispering, I'm afraid I'll hear that name. I don't, but what I do hear are words like *mother* and *prison* and *murder*. They float through the air and hover like a dark cloud.

Updating Joey's emergency contact information seemed like a simple task, but I underestimated Joy's small-town mentality. Even some of the mothers slouch in the shadows of the hallway, lolling like dogs, their thumbs flying over their phones as they too shoot dark glances my way. Their texts I imagine to be far more cutting than any words I hear from the kids: *OMG Killer Kerry's back! WTF is she wearing?* and *Her poor son!* The lead mom, the head of the pack, stands with her back against a locker, her eyes shredding me: my institution-cut hair, my supermarket clothes, my hardened face, and I'm reminded of my first time walking the prison yard, new and vulnerable, fresh meat . . . *Careful, Kerry, turn your back and she'll shank you. Or worse.*

I lower my gaze and keep moving.

Inside the school office, the secretary stands guard behind the counter. She's a round woman with puffy eyelids and a double chin. I tell her my name, and she flinches, her dark mauve lips popping into an "O" as she expels a squeaky gasp. I explain that I need to update Joey's emergency contact information. She passes me the obligatory forms and, without a word, turns and disappears through the door marked *Administration*.

I finish the forms as the secretary emerges with a middle-aged woman dressed in a navy-blue pant suit. "Mrs. Yates," the woman says. "I'm Principal Dietrich. Thank you for coming in. There are a few things we should discuss." With wet lips and shiny teeth, she explains school policy regarding parents with conviction records, more specifically felons convicted of violent crimes, and how I will not be allowed to volunteer in the school. No field trips, no classroom parties. She goes on and on as I peek at the watch dangling from the chain around her neck: 8:45.

I'm going to be late for my parole meeting with—

"Do you have any questions regarding this policy, Mrs. Yates?"

I look up. Her eyes glower with hate or fear, I'm not sure which. What does she see when she looks at me? A crazed killer? I hand over the forms and leave without a word.

If there had been any doubts, they are gone now: there will be no second chances for me in this town. No matter. I only need to hold out twenty-four months, then I'll be done with parole and completely free to take Joey and leave this town behind forever. I only have one unknown now, a fear that could dredge up my past and threaten my freedom again: Lucas.

Strange Murders: *"The Hatchet Killer"*
Transcript of the original episode, four years ago

Interview with Jack Foley, Lewis County Sheriff: The call came into dispatch at around 7:30 a.m. Early morning hikers discovered a severed leg positioned against trail marker #433 leading to Cling Back Mountain in western Lewis County. We contacted forest service personnel and met the caller at the trailhead. The leg was fully clothed and booted, severed at the hip. When I saw the way the victim's leg was staged—propped up like a mannequin leg—I knew we were looking at something more than a bear or mountain lion attack. We secured the scene and brought in a forensics crew. Later the medical examiner identified the victim as Samantha Brodie. The medical examiner's report showed that her leg had been dismembered with a hatchet. I sent search and recovery units into the area, and by noon the next day, we had recovered five more body parts. The killer was using my forest as his damn chopping block. Then came the kicker. The recovered parts didn't just belong to Ms. Brodie, but to three different women. We were looking at something evil. "A human butcher."

THREE

Adam Nash

I wait with my newly purchased cowboy boots firmly planted in the middle of a five-by-five worn patch of linoleum inside the door of the town's Justice Center, a two-story brick building at the end of Main Street. I was supposed to meet the sheriff in the entryway, but he's late getting here, or maybe I got the time wrong. I turn, bend down, and peer through the window by the door, my eyeballs shifting back and forth, surveying Joy's short and somewhat dusty main drag: a row of squatty brick buildings with various colored wood fronts, a café where Kerry used to work, a weedy green space with a red caboose, and at the very end of the street The Gold Bar, the last place Lucas Yates was seen before he disappeared.

I've stepped right into "The Hatchet Killer" episode, and Mama's voice booms in the back of my brain: *Get that damn killer, boy.*

I shake my head to keep my mother's voice away and shuffle toward the community bulletin board, immersing myself in the posted announcements: garage sales, the annual Tobacco Valley Arts Festival—Miranda, might like that—a Fourth of July Rodeo, and a notice for the weekly meeting of The Hatchet Club, dedicated to finding and bringing Lucas Yates to justice.

The door swings open, and a man steps inside sporting

Wranglers, a khaki sheriff's shirt, and gator boots with gold tipped toes. We'd never met, I'd interviewed over the phone, but before me stood Sheriff Jack Foley, dressed nearly as he had been in "The Hatchet Killer." The thrill of a full immersion swallows me as if I've been dropped directly into the *Strange Murders* episode from four years ago.

He holds out his hand and smiles, narrow eyes folding into the creases of his weathered face. "Adam?"

I extend my hand. "Sheriff Foley. Good to meet you in person." He's thinner than he looked on the show. I suck in my gut as if the camera lens is on me now as well.

"I'm late," he says. "Sorry. But we've got a hiker went missing on the PNT yesterday. Search and rescue's been working through the night. Only got a few winks myself."

I'm about to ask what PNT is, but he goes on, "Glad you're here. The last P.O. left a full case load. Couldn't get any applicants for a while, so a bit of a backlog, too. Joy isn't exactly a town most want to apply to. And then there's the other thing we discussed."

He glances quickly at me as if waiting for me to admit I've made a mistake. I smile back. He continues, "Anyway, we've shuffled some of the offenders down to Libby, but now that you're here, we can get things back to normal." His gaze shifts to the bulletin board. He curses and rips down the Hatchet Club flyer. "Come on. I'll show you around."

On the way up, he explains how the building was originally built in 1898 as a hotel, then served as a school for the deaf and blind. "After that," he says, "it sat empty for years until the village voted to revamp it as a community building. What do you think of the area so far? God's country, ain't it? You been down to The Gold Bar yet? Best damn steaks in town." He looks over his shoulder. "Not a vegetarian, are you?"

"No."

"Good. Fish?"

"Yeah. I like fish."

"No. Do you fish?"

"Haven't had much of a chance, but—"

"That's too bad. Well, here we are." He points to a door with an open transom and *Sheriff* etched in gold letters on its frosted window. "We're a satellite office," Foley explains, motioning for me to enter first. "So, we're fairly small, just a dispatcher and two officers . . . oh hey, Amber."

A thin woman, dressed in jeans and a tank top, sits in front of a large monitor behind the counter, silver and turquoise rings clicking as she types. She looks up, removes her headset, and stands. "Hey, Sheriff. Been crazy for a Monday morning so far. That missing hiker has stirred up the wackos. There's been one call after another coming in since I got here."

"Hatchet Club people." He tosses the crumpled paper onto the counter and looks at me. "That *Strange Murders* episode about Lucas Yates put our little town on the map. I heard now that the victims' families are offering a reward for Yates. A hundred grand."

The woman shakes her head. "Great. We'll have every true crime nutcase in the nation here."

The heat of exposure crawls up my neck, and I cover it with a small cough and quizzical turn of my head toward the dispatcher.

Foley blinks. "Oh, excuse me. This is Ms. Miller, our front desk and dispatcher. Adam Nash, the new PO."

She leans over the counter, blue-inked eagle wings quivering across her cleavage as she shakes my hand. "Amber, not Ms. Miller. Welcome."

I force my gaze off the eagle and upward, stammering a hello. She narrows her eyes.

Foley chuckles and claps me on the back. "Come on, Nash. I'll show you the rest of the place."

We turn down the hall, and I get a quick peek inside his office: a big desk, an oak bookcase, amazing view of the White-fish Range, then to the next office with two desks flanking a file cabinet, a small bookcase, and a dirty window over an old steam heat radiator.

"McCulley and Bird's office," he says. "They're down the hall now. Come on, I'll introduce you."

On the way he points to another door. "The loo. Just one stool, so be sure to knock."

The next door is open, a couple guys leaning over a long table. Foley introduces us. Bird looks like his name, lithe and dark, two beady eyes perched on top of chiseled cheekbones. McCulley is his anthesis. A big ole'-teddy-bear type: heavy-set, waves of brown hair, and big round eyes. They're looking at a map of the county, double-checking their grid strategy for the missing hiker search. Foley tosses out a quick introduction, exchanges a few words with them, and then we head back out to the hall.

I notice that we're almost out of hallway. "Where's my office?"

Foley rubs his chin. "Well, there's a bit of a space crunch around here, as you can see, so we've put your office downstairs for now. This way."

We go a few more steps and then take an abrupt right, which puts us on a landing to a very narrow staircase. He pulls a chain on a naked bulb, and we venture down two flights. My nose twitches from the smell of wet brick and mildew, and then finally we hit the last step. Foley pulls on another bulb, and I duck my head as we cross under a large wood beam and into a concrete block basement. Meager light floods in from a narrow band of windows running along the ceiling line. First thing I see is a large holding cell in the corner. It's empty.

Foley points to a heavy steel door. "Fire exit. It goes out to the alley. It'd be best if parolees could come through that door."

We cross to an area partitioned with portable cubicle walls arranged to make a large rectangle. Inside is a metal file cabinet and a matching dented desk paired with a swivel chair. "And here you are," he says.

I'm speechless.

"Just temporary, remember. But if things work out, we might be able to get the council to spring for some more space. Hear the Public Works folks have an extra office they're not using."

I shrug out of my jacket, toss it over the back of what must be my chair since it is the only one, and check out the mugshots pinned to the cubicle wall. "What's all this? My caseload?"

"No. Current parolees are in the file cabinet. Took the liberty of decorating for you. These are some of the county's finest." He laughs. "Reoffenders. Each and every one of these people screwed up and found themselves back in prison. Thought you could use them as an example, you know, like a deterrent for the new parolees coming in."

As if a few photos would deter criminals. I recall my time serving Chicago's 19th District and the addicts and prostitutes I'd arrested over and over. These people need jobs, housing, support. "I'm hoping to lower the recidivism rate."

"That's what the last P.O. said. He didn't last long." He sighed and rolled back on his heels. "You're seeing the Yates woman this morning, right? Sent you the file."

"That's right, but it's Grey now. She's gone back to her maiden name."

He shrugs. "A different name doesn't change anything. I give her a month, and she'll be heading back. She shouldn't have been released in the first place."

I avoid shaking my head. "Sounds like you don't believe people can change."

"Maybe other people. But this Yates woman? No one can

be married to a sicko like Lucas Yates and not be messed up. She's gonna need more than we can give her."

"True, but I'm hoping I can help her find the support she needs, she's got a kid and—"

"Sure, I get it. I admire your attitude, but . . ." he reaches into his back pocket and takes out a folded sheet of paper, "just in case it doesn't work out, here you go."

I unfold the paper and stare down at Kerry Grey's mugshot, my gut twisting with a strange brew of excitement and anxiety as Mama's voice fills my head: *Get that damn killer, boy.*

And then the scream.

Desperately shrill, it cuts through me and ignites an adrenaline surge that propels me up the back steps. Foley is on my heels. By the time we get to the first floor and to the lobby, the scream has faded to small intermittent gasps.

It's Amber, her features frozen between perplexity and horror as she stares at a large open box on her desk. McCulley and Bird are next to her. A wet penny smell coats the back of my throat. My stomach lurches.

"What's going on?" Foley asks.

No one answers, so we cross the room to look for ourselves.

I gag, cupping my hand over my mouth and nose.

"It's a leg," McCulley answers. Blood-soaked and smothered in plastic wrap, tied off like a pork loin from the butcher.

For a second, I'm dazed, my brain processing the grotesqueness, the echoed words from that episode of *Strange Murders* crystal clear in my mind: *The leg was fully clothed and booted, severed at the hip.* Heart thumping, I hunch closer, and try to tease out its secrets: Young? Old? Female? Chopped or sawed? The Hatchet Killer's work or copycat? My skin tingles.

Foley finally speaks, "Leg, my ass."

Amber stares at her boss, eyes wide. "It's not a leg?"

"Not the type you think. Get me gloves and an evidence

bag." He pulls a pen from his shirt pocket and taps the leg like a drum. *Rat-a-tat-tat.* Amber takes a breath and rushes off on her chore.

I straighten. "Mannequin."

"Uh-huh."

I look again. "The blood?"

"Animal probably," McCulley says. Bird nods in agreement. Amber reappears with the requested items. Foley snaps on gloves and reaches into the box, pulling out a folded sheet of paper. He holds it up. Five words: *He is still out there.*

Foley's gaze slides to Amber. "Where'd this package come from?"

"Building maintenance just brought it up. Said it was left downstairs by the front door. It's labeled for our department."

"I can see that." He bags the note, his jaw twitching. "Un-frickin'-believable. Like I don't know he's still out there."

He turns to McCulley. "Process this stuff. See if there are any prints." Then to me. "Kerry Yates's release is stirring things up around here. I want you to figure out what that woman knows about her husband, understood? I intend to find Lucas and then I'm going to see them both back in prison."

I swallow back the sour spit pooled inside my cheeks and nod, my gaze slowly moving to the wall clock as its blurry hands tick off another minute: 8:45. Kerry will be here soon. And after all this time, I'm finally going to meet the killer's wife.

I'm getting closer, Mama.

Strange Murders: *"The Hatchet Killer"*
Transcript of the original episode, four years ago

Interview with Leeza Dixon, former District Attorney, retired:
Mrs. Yates was pulled over on suspicion of DUI. The officers
saw an open container of alcohol in her vehicle, providing
probable cause for a lawful search in which they discovered the
severed finger inside a shopping bag on the floorboard of the
back seat. The appendage was later matched to what would be
determined as the third victim, Abby Marshal. No prints were
found on the shopping bag, and there was nothing else to tie
Mrs. Yates to the crimes. She maintained her innocence right
up to the sentencing, where she received six years for Accessory
Felon After the Fact. Do I think she helped kill those women?
Why, yes, I do. I only wish we could have proved it.

FOUR

Adam Nash

She looks nothing like her mugshot, or the actress who portrayed her on *Strange Murders*. She's small, maybe a little over five feet with good enough features and an intense gaze. That's what's missing in the mugshot. An intensity to her eyes despite imprisonment, or maybe because of it.

"Kerry Grey?" All the right inflection in my voice, as if I don't know who she is, haven't been researching her for weeks and wondering about her for the last two years.

She nods and gives me a look that says she already thinks I'm a jerk and settles onto the torn orange vinyl cushion of a chair that I'd pulled out of a storage. She doesn't seem to notice the room, if you can even call it that, more like a dank alcove in a musty dungeon. After four years in a prison cell, guess it looks okay to her.

I introduce myself and we begin powering through the mandatory paperwork. I explain a few of the rules, finishing with an explanation about surprise home visits and required drug testing.

"I don't do drugs."

"Good. All your tests will come back negative then." I write a note and pass it to her. "The clinic is down the street. They'll be expecting you."

We talk about employment, and she says she's okay for a little while, she lives with her grandfather and he provides the basics, food and stuff, for both her and her son, Joey. Her voice softens a bit when she says her son's name. I've found her vulnerability.

"How's it for you at home?" I lean in closer, yearning for the personal details to satisfy my real needs. A mistake. She leans back.

"Home's fine." Lips tight.

I swallow back my anticipation, go on as if each question is innocent, each answer satisfying. "You live with your grandfather. Callan is his name, right?"

"Yes."

"And your son, Joey? Where's your mother?"

"She's not in the picture. Hasn't been for years."

I nod. I knew this, but I make a note anyway, my eyes on the paper now, casual, disinterested. "Do you have friends? A church family maybe?"

"Pops is a regular churchgoer. Not me so much."

I fiddle with my pen. "You've been gone a while. It can't be easy to adjust to the outside world. Things change, people change."

"My son's changed. He's ten now." A crack in her veneer— again about her son—as she looks at her hands. "I've missed four years of his life."

"There's still a lot of time with him. He's young. And he'll be looking to you as a role model." I use her son as a lever, hoping for a wider opening.

She shifts from pensive back to a prison-hardened callousness. Reality is tough and she gets it. "I was in prison. What's there to look up to?"

"You're out. Starting over. It takes a lot of courage and hard work to start over and achieve your dreams. That's what he'll learn from you." By rote from the parole officer's handbook, but it seems to work.

She fidgets with the hem of her shirt.

"You do have dreams, don't you, Kerry?"

"Just nightmares."

I'm not sure if she means that literally or if she sees her future as some sort of ugly joke. Probably both. "Tell me about prison." Her eyes dart up and I quickly add, "The programs you completed, that type of stuff." Back to the book. Cover the mandatory topics, drug testing, employment possibilities, goals . . . but I feel my throat tighten around the words as Mother's voice penetrates my thoughts: *Find that damn killer.*

"Got my GED and took a few courses in computers."

"Did you like working with computers?"

"No. Not really."

"What's something you're good at?"

"Surviving."

"That's important."

"Yeah."

"What's surviving look like going forward?"

"Staying the hell out of prison."

I point at Foley's handiwork. "These folks said the same thing."

She squints.

"Reoffenders," I tell her. "All of them sent back."

She looks away.

The lines on the form are full now, but I've come up empty. My chest clenches as I see Mother glaring at an incompetent cop on *Strange Murders,* cigarette smoke curling around her head. And this time I see that cop on the tube is me. *Ask her, Adam!*

"Lucas," I say.

A deep sigh. She'd known it was coming. "What about him?"

"He's what got you there in the first place."

I sit back, fold my hands. The truth swells, pulses to be released, and I give her the space to satisfy that urge. *Let it all out, Kerry. You need to vent.* But she says nothing. The only clue to her feelings is the glint in her eyes. Anger. Or maybe amusement. *This guy's out to get me, but I'm smarter, I won't fall for his crap trap.*

"Lucas," she finally says. "I don't know where he is if that's what you're thinking. If I knew, I'd find him and—"

"And?"

She shifts.

"And what, Kerry?"

"He cost me my son's childhood. And more. He was a mistake."

"Your Rubicon."

Her brows knit together and her forehead crinkles, just like Miranda's brows do sometimes. I cringe and shake off thoughts of my wife and all our problems. No time for that now.

"Rubicon," I explain. "The point of no return. Some decisions are like that. Once you make them, there's no going back."

She breathes slow and deep. I mirror her breath and can feel her remembering the moment of that decision, in a drunken haze, or not, a hot summer night, or winter's chill, under the stars, or in a cheap room, I have no idea, but I do know that one moment of mislaid passion, that one single decision, can make all the difference. It has in Kerry's life. It has in mine.

I keep my voice calm and convincing. "A part of you thinks he might show up."

She meets my gaze. I've hit on something. *What is it? What aren't you telling me, Kerry?*

I think I know. Lucas is a former marine, a man who's killed for his country, killed for his own pleasure, and then eluded the cops for four years. He's smart, skilled, determined, and not the type to simply let go of something. Especially not his wife and kid.

"Have you heard from him yet?"

She lowers her head, stares at the floor, dark hair veiling her eyes. "No."

But she will. She knows it and so do I.

Not even two minutes after Kerry leaves, Amber invades my dingy space. The smell of Kerry's desperation still hangs in the air, and what I really want is a few moments alone to absorb the afterglow of our conversation and diffuse the emotional storm left in her wake. Amber has a different agenda.

"That leg this morning. Foley's still mad about it. Furious, actually. Those Hatchet Club folks get under his skin." She flops in the chair across from me and sets down the can of Red Bull she had clutched in her hand. She tips her head back, unscrews the lid on a tiny bottle taken from her pocket, and disperses two drops in each eye before nodding toward the outside door. "So, what was she like?"

I shrug. "Seems pretty normal, for the most part."

"Normal? That's how you describe her? She carries dead people's fingers around in shopping bags. Ask me, 'normal' isn't quite the right word."

"Who's taking care of dispatch right now?"

"I'm taking a potty break. McCulley's covering for me. It's been a hell of a morning dispatching reserve deputies for search and rescue, and that leg thing . . . I deserve a break, don't you think? What the Yates woman tell you?" she says, back to Kerry again. "That she's innocent? Didn't know anything about her husband killing those women?"

"Yup. That pretty much sums it up."

"There were three of them, you know. They didn't stand a chance against a man like Lucas. And now we've got this missing hiker. What if . . .?" She shudders.

I stand and pick up a file folder I'd pulled earlier from back-logged cases hoping she'll get the hint and remove herself from the chair still warm from Kerry. "Terrible thing. Hope they find her. Bet her family is worried."

"Her parents are on their way. Should be here anytime. You're from Chicago, right?"

"Yup."

"Dangerous place, I hear."

"Can be."

"Yeah, well, we got our own type of danger around here. These woods . . . it's like they're alive somehow. Evil." She guzzles down the rest of her Red Bull, crushes the can, and tosses it at my wastebasket. It misses, clinks on the floor, and slides under my desk. She bends to retrieve it, her shirt sagging. The eagle takes flight.

She glances up, catches me looking. "You must be fascinated with Liberty?"

"Excuse me?"

She draws a red nail across the curve of her chest. "My tat." She laughs.

Embarrassment gushes through me and my gaze sinks, fixating on a crack in the concrete, and it's like I'm fourteen again, my mother's voice cutting through my brain, *What are you looking at, Adam?* I slammed my laptop shut, too late. She'd seen the screen, the naked woman and the man doing dirty things to her. I was mortified, and the disappointment in Mother's voice was unbearable, *You're just like all the rest of them.* I vowed right then to never let Mother down again.

I clear my throat. "I'm sorry. Your tattoo . . . it's hard not to notice."

"Good art should be noticed, don't you think?" She bites her bottom lip and I look away.

As if it was art she wanted seen.

Ding. I look down at my phone. A text from Miranda. A single letter: O.

Amber is still talking. "Pony over on Fifth did it."

"Pony?"

"Don't laugh. Pony Malloy. He's good. A real artist. I'm saving for another. A coiled snake on my ankle. You inked?"

"No." I'm stuck on my wife's text: O. Her code for ovulating. Our fertility window, she calls it. Baby-making time. For a week every month, it's like this. At first, I thought it would be great. What guy wouldn't? Guaranteed sex. But now all I can think is: Why tonight?

"Oh yeah, why not?"

I look up. "Excuse me?"

Amber squints. "Why don't you have a tat? Afraid of the pain?"

"Pain?"

Ding. Another text: ETS

My wife's code for: Estimated Time of Sex. Miranda is a planner.

"Of the needle," Amber says.

I scratch my head, confused, wondering where this conversation is going, the muddle of needles and sex destroying my focus.

She stands up and walks over to me. "Fear of the needle is common, you know. Pony's seen it a lot. Even Yates was afraid."

"Lucas? Pony inked him?"

"That's right." Her voice is softer, eyes tiny blue slits under lids heavy with black mascara. She's standing right in front of me now. "Pony inked the Hatchet Killer, back when he was just Lucas Yates." She leans forward, pulling her shirt down just a little. "An eagle, just like this one."

My eyes go wide, fixate, and something stirs down below. I shudder, all warm blood and tingles. After a couple seconds, I peel my gaze away, glance at the time on my phone, and reply to my wife: ETS 6:00.

Strange Murders: *"The Hatchet Killer"*
Transcript of the original episode, four years ago

Interview with Bob Kenny, Owner of The Gold Bar Casino, Joy, Montana: I remember Lucas that night. He was with Kerry, and they were dancing together, and it looked like everything was fine between them. But later around eleven, I saw Kerry alone at the bar, upset about something and slamming back one drink after another. I cut her off early. But after my shift, when I was leaving, she was in the corner of the lot talking to someone. It was too dark to tell who it was, but it looked like they were arguing. Heard later that she'd been pulled over and they found that finger in her vehicle.

FIVE

Kerry Grey

I exit the clinic with my head down.

The whole drug test thing was humiliating, squatting over a cup, willing my pee to hit the mandatory fill line while the tech stood by and watched. Turns out the only thing flowing was a one-sided conversation. Hers.

"Chrissie VanElst," she'd announced. "We were in gym class together sophomore year, maybe you remember me, short hair, braces?"

I looked up from my cup at her current face—long hair and beautiful smile—and shook my head.

"Sophomore English class," she added.

And it all came flooding back, not the pee, but the memories.

It had started in English class with an invitation. Chrissie was never popular. Neither was I, so I should have expected something when we both got invited to a party that night. We gathered down by the river bottom around a blazing bonfire, passing a bottle of wine between us. The popular crowd, the pretty ones, the girls with the perfect clothes, perfect hair, perfect boyfriends, and here we were, all of us partying together, seventeen and full of ourselves, full of alcohol, too. That's when they turned on us. Sly comments and little taunts at first, then it escalated. *Killer Kerry* could take it, and, with me being no fun to pick on, they turned all their bullying on Chrissie who didn't stand a chance. And me, I didn't try to help her or defend her either. Instead, I sat by like a timid shadow and let it all happen, just glad the focus was off me. I may have even pretended to laugh. I remember her eyes flicked to me once, begging for support. I'd turned away. After Chrissy ran off in tears, I walked home feeling sick from the booze, but sicker from the fact that I betrayed myself and all that Pops had raised me to be. I never did go back to school after that, never saw Chrissy again, and by the middle of that summer, I was pregnant and full-time at the café.

"I'm married now," Chrissie said. "We've got three kids and we're very happy." She tilted her chin, her gaze sliding down my nose and fixating on the cup between my legs. She smirked. "Life takes us in different directions, I guess."

As I now cross the clinic lot I think of her words "different directions" and am glad she's found a level and clear path through life. My path plunged me over a cliff and landed me in the state prison. I try to shake off my sullen thoughts when I hear engines roaring in the distance. As they grow closer, I shield my eyes and squint down Highway 93. The first ATV rolls into sight, mud-caked and spitting puffs of blue smoke from its exhaust. Three more follow, then a couple more, all heading into the adjacent lot. They circle in front of the door to The Gold Bar Casino, a place popular with bikers who come through the area for one last chance to drink and blow money before crossing the border into British Columbia. One of them breaks away from the group and comes my way. I squint, an uneasy feeling creeping over me. Someone else from my past?

He comes closer and takes off his helmet. It's Wyatt Jones.

I should be prepared for this. I knew I'd see him sooner or

later. But what's the protocol for meeting a guy you dumped years ago? Hug him? Shake his hand? I opt for something easy. I smile. He doesn't and my smile slips off like water on oil.

"I heard you were back," he says, his tone flat.

"Just got back yesterday."

"Good."

Only it's not a happy *good*, but a disinterested *good*. Or maybe a cautious *good*. A slight frown hints he is unsure himself. I nod toward the casino parking lot. "What are you doing?"

"Volunteering part-time with search and rescue. We've been in the woods since daybreak looking for a lost hiker."

"Oh. I heard helicopters this morning."

He nods. "A college girl. She's been missing since yesterday, but we're hopeful that we'll find her."

It's always good to be hopeful, I guess. But as long as I can remember, the Kootenai has claimed its share of hikers. It swallows its victims whole, alive, and plump, and after the search has died down and winter's cold and summer's heat have feasted on them, and their names have become only a faint whisper in the lips of the wind, it spits out their decayed carcasses. This girl doesn't stand a chance out there.

Is it possible that Lucas's corpse is rotting under those pines? Or did he bend over this hiker's form, fulfilling his hungry need to kill? Was that him last night, lurking outside the cabin, watching Joey's window, waiting to—

"I can't imagine what it was like for you in prison."

My skin prickles. I shake off my thoughts and his question. "Time seems to have treated you okay." Did that sound like flirting?

He runs his hand through his light brown hair. Lucas had dark hair. Dark as night.

"I've been fine," he says. "It was hard when Mom died, but I've adjusted, I guess."

"Your mother passed? I didn't know." A memory zips through my mind: Lynn Jones giving me a disapproving and snarky once-over. "I'm so sorry, Wyatt." Although, she never liked me. Never wanted her son slumming around with *that* girl. The one without a mother, without a proper outfit, without . . . whatever. I always came up short in her eyes. Still, I'm sorry she's dead, at least for his sake.

I look around, fidget with my truck keys, and after a couple awkward beats, he sighs and points to the casino. "Do you have a little time?"

They call it a casino, but the Gold Bar is really a dark saloon with a dozen video poker games glowing from the corner. A half-dozen guys line the bar, their focus on a large-screen television broadcasting updates on the missing hiker.

Wyatt moves to the back room to where the search team members are gathered, but I don't want to intrude, so I stop, planning to wait here until he returns. I listen to the news update: *The search continues for a missing woman originally from California. The county forest service reports that Allison Turner, a twenty-three-year-old University of Montana grad student, was last seen around noon on Sunday, May 23, on the Pacific Northwest Trail. Turner, unfamiliar with the area, was hiking with her boyfriend when he fell and was injured approximately three miles northeast of the Webb Mountain Lookout Tower. Turner took off to get help, but in the meantime, other hikers found her boyfriend and were able to get him to a nearby ranger station. Lewis County authorities transported the boyfriend who is currently hospitalized and in stable condition. Turner's vehicle was found still parked at the trailhead. Ground search efforts are underway, and Two Bear Air continues to sweep the region with an infrared unit. The area is dangerously rugged and covered in dense forests. If you know anything, authorities want to hear from you.*

"Hope to hell the Hatchet Killer didn't get her."

My gaze swivels to a couple guys at the end of the bar. They're eyeing me. One of them tips his Stetson my way. Then a raspy heckle erupts from an old woman perched on a stool in front of a blackjack machine, a drag-along oxygen tank sitting next to her like an obedient dog. "Hatchet Killer," she says. "Saw his ghost 'bout two weeks ago up on Cutter Ridge."

Stetson man laughs. "The only ghost you seen, Nettie, is the one that says booooze."

She salutes them with her beer bottle, arm skin jiggling. "That's right, baby. You joke all you want, but I know what I saw. It was his ghost, I'm telling ya. Big guy, long hair, he looked just like he did on that show 'cept he was wearing nothing but a loincloth. And his hatchet, 'course."

"Sounds like your smut dream, Nettie," one of them says, sliding a gaze my way.

Ick. I wheel and head to the back room where Wyatt is bent over a map with a couple of his team members, tracing their fingers along invisible paths, speculating on the hiker. Done for the day, but unable to give up the chase, or hope, of finding the woman alive.

Wyatt introduces me to the group. I get some hard stares and then a bit of stupidity: "You don't look anything like you did on the show."

Wyatt rolls his eyes. One guy shrugs at me, like he's sorry or something, the others return their gazes to the map, my presence forgotten for the moment. Or they're ignoring me. They know who I am. Killer Kerry's back in town and suddenly a hiker is missing. Coincidence? Makes me wonder when the sheriff will come knocking.

Wyatt doesn't seem to notice. He motions for me to come closer. "Take a look," he says. "Burlington Northern brought in a mobile cell tower, so we're able to coordinate through the Sheriff's Department, but we've got nothing so far. It's like she vanished."

I point at a marked spot on the map. "Ground zero?"

"Yeah. That's where the boyfriend injured himself. They managed to get this far back on the trail before he couldn't go any farther. She left him here and, according to him, headed this way on the trail." He traces a line south to the trailhead. "Their car was parked here."

"They were only a couple miles from their car," one of the other guys says. "We can't figure out why she didn't just follow the trail."

I lean over and take a good look at the search grid as Wyatt explains, "Another group came through that afternoon and found the guy. They went for help. He was airlifted to Libby. Minor injuries. A broken leg's about it."

I'm still looking at the map. Something seems off.

Wyatt goes on, "Foot patrol started the search here and moved outward, covered over twenty-seven square miles so far. Dog teams are on it. Forest service and Flight for Life Choppers have joined in. Airborne has swept the whole region. Infrared units, too. No trace. Nothing."

My mind churns. I'd done this hike before. The trail runs upward and then along a gut-like dip in the mountain over a glacier-formed basin lake. It's steep and this time of year, it'd be iced-packed at the higher elevations, but it's well marked.

I trace a thin squiggly blue line on the map. "Even if she got off trail at some point, she would have hit Russ Creek here."

One of the guys agrees. "She wouldn't have crossed it. No sane person would. I saw it. It's running hard and fast. Spring melt-off."

I venture, "Okay. So, let's say she was smart enough not to attempt to cross it. All she had to do was follow the creek down the mountain."

"I thought the same thing. We've searched that whole area."

I shake my head. "It doesn't look good, does it? Either she tried to cross Russ Creek and got washed away, or something got to her. A bear maybe," I quickly add. Grizzlies frequent these parts, everyone knows that. But I look up from the map, past Wyatt's troubled gaze, and my heart sinks as I see their accusing stares. The comment from the guy at the bar echoes in my mind: *Hope to hell the Hatchet Killer didn't get her.*

After a while, Wyatt and I retreat to a corner booth with a pizza and drinks. Once we're alone, his mood turns somber.

"Can't believe it's been four years," he says. "I wrote to you. Tried to visit, but you . . . I don't know, you never . . . you just cut me off. You ghosted me. Is that even possible from prison?"

He sort of laughs, but I know he's serious. I hurt him. His letters had been full of concern and genuine interest in "helping" me. I didn't need his help. Or his pity.

"Four years is a long time not to answer my letters, Kerry."

"I know. I'm sorry. It's just that I couldn't answer . . . after I . . ."

I didn't deserve his affections and he knew it and he knew why: We'd grown up together and were best friends, sometimes more, and he always talked about us being together forever. But then I met Lucas. Lucas: those dark dangerous eyes that swallow you whole like the forest, so exciting, and oh, so enticing. I just didn't realize that the "danger" was so real. Wyatt, even though he felt betrayed, stood by me through everything. And those letters from Wyatt?—Sweet and caring words, but with a deep vein of hurt running through them.—They stung, knowing how I'd had a chance with him, been stupid with Lucas, and screwed up every good thing in my life.

"I never thought you did it," he says.

I swipe my mouth. "What do you mean?"

"You know what I mean."

I toss the crumpled napkin onto my plate and look toward the door. I thought we were supposed to have some pizza and catch up, not discuss my crime by association and resulting prison time. *I need an excuse to get out of here.*

"Remember the cat out on the ice that spring?" he asks.

"The cat? I don't know. Maybe. What are you talking about?"

"We must've been around eleven, twelve maybe. We met by The Res, you remember, like we used to do."

"Uh, huh."

"There was a cat stranded out there on the ice. Poor thing. Mewing like a wounded rabbit, all tangled up in some fishing line."

It was coming back. "It was your cat. The orange one."

"Yeah, that's right, it was. Never could figure out how it got out there in the first place. You could have died rescuing that stupid cat, but you still went after it."

Spring, the ice was melting. The cat was practically hog-tied in old fishing line, slipping and sliding on the ice, struggling to get free. Wyatt was already there, watching from the bank, not moving, sort of frozen with shock. I got there and saw the cat and knew it was only a matter of time before it broke through the ice.

"That's why I know you didn't do what everyone says you did."

I tense. "And what exactly is that?"

"That you helped Lucas hack those women up. You know, like gutting a deer."

Killer Kerry. Killer Kerry. Killer . . .

"Kerry. You okay?"

"Yeah."

He pats my arm and then keeps his hand there. Heat surges

through me. How long has it been since a man has touched me?

"I'm sorry," he says. "I shouldn't have said it like that. Didn't mean to upset you." His thumb traces circles on my skin.

"No. I'm fine. Really." My breath is ragged. I should pull my arm away, but I don't, and the way his finger moves over my skin, in little circles, firm but not too much pressure as if an unconscious movement that reflects his circling thoughts.

"How is Joey? He must be so happy that you're home."

I blink and clear my throat. "He's not talking much. He's distant, angry inside, and it . . . it scares me." Truth is, I don't know how to talk to Joey about anything, not really, and it hurts. "And me coming home has just got people talking more. It's hard on him. No kid should have to go through all this. I'm just so angry with Lucas, you know? I have these fantasies of finding him and making him pay for . . . for everything."

"You probably could."

"Could what?"

"Find him. You know the mountains around here. Enough time, enough help, and you could find him."

I don't know how to respond. He *wants* me to find him? Or wants to *help*? He doesn't need me. He knows these mountains as well as I do. Is he after the reward money like those crazy Hatchet Club people? Not likely a reason for Wyatt considering his family's fortunes. Then what? I shrug, uncertain and uncomfortable. "Lucas is long gone. Crossed over the border, probably somewhere up in Canada living the good life."

"Do you really believe that?"

"I don't know. I want to believe it, I guess." I recall the flicker of light. Moonlight reflecting off animals' eyes, Pops had said, but—

"People think they've seen him in the Kootenai."

Yeah, people like Nettie. Half-drunk, half-crazed.

"It's okay to be scared. Anyone would be." His gaze intensifies. "I would do anything to protect you, you know that, right?"

He's still caressing my arm, but his movements are slower now, more deliberate. I lean forward, my pulse throbbing, and I'm dizzy, floating in my chair, my body remembering what my mind has worked to shut out for so long.

I struggle to find my voice. "I . . . I should go. Joey's out of school soon and . . ."

I pull back my hand and slide out of the booth.

He rises slowly and stares down at me. "I'll be here whenever you need me."

Strange Murders: *"The Hatchet Killer"*
Transcript of the original episode, four years ago

Camera shot panning Main Street and the surrounding mountains.

Show host, Wesley Steele (voiceover): Joy, Montana, home of the Hatchet Killer, Lucas Yates, to all appearances is a tiny village nestled in the Rocky Mountains, just a stone's throw from the Canadian Border. Picturesque and inviting, with a community of nearly fifteen hundred hardy residents, able to endure record low temperatures and abundant snow. From any point in town one can see the majestic Whitefish Mountains, fish the Tobacco River, hike the Pacific Northwest Trail, see an abundance of wildlife, and live a simple life. To many, Joy, Montana is nothing less than paradise. But thanks to Lucas Yates, to a few unfortunate souls it became hell on earth. My question for viewers is, how well do you know your own town, the people there, your own neighbors? If we can't be safe from the bloody blade of a hatchet in a pristine place like Joy, are we safe anywhere?

SIX

Adam Nash

I hover in the kitchen door and watch my wife bustle about, cupboards thumping, drawers sliding as she reaches and bends, searching and concentrating, her forehead scrunching until a crease forms between her clear blue eyes.

Aw . . . the crease, *the eleven*, I call it—two parallel vertical lines smack dab between the brows. The first time I noticed it was in a bar on Halsted, not too far from Wrigley Field. I was out with the guys after a shift; they were helping me drink away the residual effects of a failed relationship, one of many that had ended badly. Somewhere between my first and fourth beer, I swore off women. But by drink number five, Miranda walked in the door. Long blond hair pulled back, red lipstick and pencil-thin heels. She was beautiful, and I changed my mind just like that.

One of the guys leaned over and whispered. "Way out of your league. You'll never be able to give her what she wants."

I took it as a dare and approached her. But the whole time we talked, I figured I'd lost that dare. She was gorgeous, smart, too perfect for me. Yet, she hung on my every word, a number eleven forming between her brows as she focused, yes, paid attention and even asked questions about me wanting to be a cop. She was interested.

As was I.

A year later when she said "yes," my friend's words echoed in my mind, "You'll never be able to give her what she wants."

I laughed it off, cocky enough to believe that all she really wanted was me. I was wrong. Miranda had a whole list of wants: a big wedding, an exotic honeymoon, a condo in the Wicker Park neighborhood. Then came the next "want"—a baby to fill that time when I apparently neglected her, working my butt off to get her all the other things she wanted in life.

That's when I learned my friend was right after all. I couldn't give her *everything* she wanted. We went to a fertility specialist; I was the problem. Turns out that stress causes low sperm count. Being a cop was stressful. Keeping up with Miranda's wants was stressful.

Miranda decided we needed a drastic lifestyle change. And here we are, sixteen hundred miles from Chicago and no closer to her goal.

She looks up and catches me lurking near the stairs. The eleven disappears and her eyes sparkle. "There you are. Get over here, Adam. I've been waiting for you."

Her voice is warm and inviting and my heart soars, even though I know why she's being so sweet. And I feel like a fraud. She thinks I've made a big compromise for her. That I gave up my dream job as a Chicago cop and moved out here, to Big Sky country, fresh mountain air, open spaces, a low-stress job, just to please her. To give her what she wants. To make a baby. But nothing is further from the truth.

I smile at my wife and cross to the kitchen bar, nodding at the bottles there. "Wine?"

"I forgot to tell you. I met the neighbors."

My stomach churns.

"I asked them to stop by later for a glass of wine, or two."

No, no, no. I'd counted on some time for myself, in the attic later. "Tonight? Really? But . . . you know . . ." I draw a circle in the air in the shape of a giant "O" and flash what I hope is a sexy grin.

"That's at six o'clock." Another crinkle between the brows—What *are* you thinking, Adam? "I told them to arrive between eight-thirty and nine o'clock."

Worked out down to the minute. "Oh." I shrug, slide out of my jacket and toss it onto the counter.

Her expression turns coy. "I found the smoothie maker."

"Great."

She scoops fruit into the mixer, then yogurt and starts adding a handful of leafy spinach, walnuts . . . her mixture of a male fertility-smoothie. I've been gagging them down for months.

"How did your first day go?" she asks, glances at the clock: 5:20. Smiles.

Forty minutes to ETS. I sigh.

She eyes my jacket, not waiting for my answer. "What's this?" She pulls the folded paper from my pocket.

I tense. "Work stuff."

Her eyes narrow. "Oh yeah?" She wipes her hand on a dish-towel and opens it, chewing her lower lip as she reads, then grimaces. "Weird News Online? This doesn't seem like your usual reading."

I shrug. Nonchalant, cool . . . but my heart jackhammers. "It's written about my first parolee."

She skims it again. "You saw this woman today . . . Kerry Yates?"

"Kerry Grey now. She took back her maiden name."

"Who wouldn't? Her husband's a killer."

She squints. The eleven is back.

I squirm, stare at the counter. *Stay calm. Keep it casual.* She despises *Strange Murders.* Never watched it. Hates it when

I watch it. I'd never admit to her that when this position posted to the national job board, I applied straight away, precisely because of Kerry Grey. Precisely because of this case.

She tosses the article aside and goes back to the smoothie, finishing with pumpkin seeds and goji berries. "Do you believe her?"

"How's that?"

"That she didn't know. I mean, how could she not have known her own husband was a serial killer? Wouldn't she have noticed something? Odd behavior? Blood on his clothing? Something? He chopped up women. How do you miss that?"

Yes, yes, how do you miss that? "I don't think that really matters at this time. She's paid her debt to society. I need to make sure she doesn't screw up and go back to prison." I tap the article. "This doesn't mention the child she and Lucas had together. A boy. He's ten now."

"*She* has a child?" A sigh. A roll of her eyes. "Figures. Some women don't deserve what they get."

Her voice snips with jealousy. And we are back to the reason we moved here—at least her reason—and it turns my stomach worse than the globs of greens visible in the glass cylinder. "Can't you at least feel sorry for the kid, Miranda?"

"Sounds like you're more worried about her family than me."

"It's my job," I snap back, then regret it.

The eleven reappears, dancing angrily between her brows. It reminds me of the way Mother used to look at me when I tracked up the floor, forgot to get her cigs at the corner market . . . asked for something to eat.

"I'm sorry," I say, then pause as she jabs the start button on the blender. The blades chew through fruity flesh and tender leaves, grind nuts to grit. She pours it into a tall glass and hands it to me.

Her face smooths. "No. I'm sorry. It's . . ." She looks down, black lashes fanned out over creamy skin. Her sweet and vulnerable act.

"What, dear?" I play along. No need to invite conflict.

She bats her lashes. "I don't think this is ever going to happen. And when I hear about women like . . . like Kerry Yates who—"

"It's going to happen for us." I put my smoothie down, cross over to her, and take her in my arms. I pull her close and murmur dirty things against her lips, playful and promising, but inside, I sigh. *Let's just get this done.*

I roll off and stare at the ceiling, breathing hard.

"I know it's going to work this month," Miranda says, rubbing her belly. She lays next to me, in her position, pillow under her hips, just the right angle for the little spermies to swim to meet their fate, swallowed into her greedy, waiting egg.

Twilight spills through the slats in our miniblinds, her lips are rubbed red from my kisses and spread tight over white even teeth as she speaks, "This move, this house . . . I can't believe you did this all for me. It's everything I've ever wanted."

I think of the day the cameras focused on Mama, her calling me her "little armchair detective" and my interview this morning with Kerry. *Everything I've always wanted.* I smile and Miranda responds with a grin, nestles next to me, satisfied and ignorant.

Strange Murders: *"The Hatchet Killer"*
Transcript of the original episode, four years ago

Interview with Sheriff Foley: After finding that leg, I called in maybe a half-dozen or so cadaver dog teams. I knew we were up against something big. We searched a two-mile grid that afternoon, pulling out body parts nestled in the forest floor like someone had set up a damn Humpy Dumpty Easter egg hunt with bits and pieces of Yate's victims. Took the medical examiner another six months to get everyone put back together again.

SEVEN

Adam Nash

Marco and Rachel, our neighbors, are in their early thirties. He's a man's man, works construction, and, with a quick and condescending appraisal of my less-than-muscular frame, has already offered to help with anything that needs to be fixed around the house.

Rachel backs him up. "You can use him any time you need. Just holler," she says. "There is nothing he can't fix." She says this with a glint in her eye.

My wife giggles and holds out her glass for a refill. I oblige and look at Marco: dark, built like a block with a strong chin and sure smile. There's no way he's coming over to fix anything of mine.

I uncork a third bottle and by the time the sun sets on our little party, I'm half-drunk. We're all half-drunk.

And that's when the trouble starts.

Miranda lights the tiki torches. This morning she struggled to find our smoothie maker, and now she's found tiki torches, and throws a party with *amazing* tapas, as Rachel keeps saying.

Many things are amazing to Rachel: the tapas, the wine, the way Miranda and I are so obviously soul mates. She notices these things in couples, she says, it's her job, she's a therapist specializing in marriage counseling. She's spent the last five years getting to know her patients and what they need to make their relationships work.

"Obviously, you two are good together," she says about Miranda and me. "I can tell by the little things. Like how you look at each other. You have amazing eye contact."

Miranda and I glance at each other and immediately look away, then laugh.

"No seriously," Rachel says. "There's been several studies to show that couples with strong eye contact have a more intimate and meaningful relationship. I can spot it the first time a couple walks into my office. No eye contact, and I know there's something missing at the core of their relationship. Part of my therapy includes having the couple stare into one another's eyes for four minutes. It's a powerful exercise."

"How's that?" Miranda leans into the conversation.

"Well . . . they say that four minutes is all it takes for two people to fall in love." She reaches out for me to top off her glass, her skirt inching up her thigh. "But what I find with my couples is that it lowers defensiveness, increases vulnerability, and makes for better relations in the bedroom."

Miranda straightens up and looks my way. *Great.* Now we'll be adding a staring contest to next month's scheduled roll-on-demand. I recork the bottle and set it aside.

"That type of work must be rewarding," I say. "Helping couples in trouble. Saving marriages."

She nods. "I do like to help people. You must feel the same way. Miranda said that you left police work for parole. That you want to make a difference in people's lives, rather than just arrest them over and over."

"True." *Sort of.*

She looks straight into my eyes. "I admire that."

One one-thousand, two one-thousand . . .

I blink and keep talking. "I worked vice for almost five

years, arresting mostly dealers and sex workers. Sometimes I'd see them back on the street the same day, doing the same thing. The problems ran so much deeper than what the system could deal with, what I could deal with."

Eight one-thousand, nine one-thousand . . .

Miranda clears her throat. "And now he's dealing with criminals trying to . . . how did you put it earlier, honey? Pay their debts to society. Like that Kerry Yates."

Rachel breaks eye contact and looks around the table. "No. Is that true? I knew she was out . . . I just didn't put it together that you would be her . . . I went to school with her."

I feel my breath catch.

Marco sets aside his own wine glass and has his hand back on his wife's knee. "Who's Kerry Yates?"

"Someone who's definitely in need of a marriage fix," Rachel answers and then laughs at her own joke. "Haven't you heard of Lucas Yates?"

Marco scrunches his beefy brow.

Rachel clues him in. "The Hatchet Killer."

"*His* wife?"

"Yes." Rachel bobs her head Marco's way. "*His* wife." Then goes on to say that she knew Kerry but didn't exactly hang out with her after school or anything. And she can't quite remember if Kerry did any sports in high school or not, but she was sort of the outdoorsy type, you know how they are, fishing and hunting of all things. "Sort of a loner." She adds with a shrug, "Of course those types usually are. They didn't mention that on *Strange Murders*."

I lean forward, all ears, willing her to go on and she does.

"And really, the actress who they picked to portray her was a total miss. Did you see that episode?" she asks Miranda.

Miranda looks dazed. "She was on *Strange Murders*?"

"Yes, yes." Rachel looks like an eager puppy.

"True crime shows aren't really my thing," Miranda says, looking my way. "But I bet Adam has seen it."

Miranda's angry now. "It's sort of part of my job to watch it," I offer, but I know it won't cover the simmering boil in my wife.

"That's so cool," Rachel gushes. "Have you met her yet?"

"I have, but I can't talk—"

"Of course not. I wouldn't dream of asking you to divulge anything. Professional privileged information and all. But you've got to admit, that actress on the show doesn't look a bit like her. The real Kerry is much prettier."

Miranda sits back, arms crossed.

Rachel goes on, "She always was pretty. In a natural way, though, not exactly beautiful. But she caught Wyatt Jones's attention back then. He was the most popular guy in school. We never could figure out what he saw in her. His family is big around here, ranchers, thousands and thousands of acres. One of the original families to settle the area." She rubs the tips of her fingers together. "Big money, know what I mean?"

"Kerry's family lives modestly, I take it."

"Dirt poor."

"Did you know Lucas?" I ask.

"No. He wasn't from around here and older than us by a few years. He'd just got out of the service, maybe Army, I can't remember, but he was a big guy in the military, got some sort of medal."

Marines, but I don't correct her. She's on a roll.

Marco draws a circle around his ear. "That explains it. Combat trauma. Bet that's why he kills now. A lot of guys come back messed up."

Rachel drains the rest of her wine. "Doubtful. Childhood trauma would be my guess. Some sort of issue with his mother. That's why he targets women. Obviously, the mutilation suggests deep-seated anger."

Marco laughs. "My wife, the criminal profiler. Too much crime TV, honey." Then to us, "She lives and breathes true crime."

My brain buzzes. I lock eyes with Rachel. One one-thousand, two one-thousand . . .

Rachel slowly disengages and gives Marco's arm a playful slap. "Anyway, Kerry was dating Wyatt when Lucas came to town. Rumor is that he came into the café where she worked almost every day. Pursued her hard. She eventually fell for him and broke up with Wyatt. About a month later, the word got around that she was getting married. They had a kid right away." She smirks just a bit, gossip isn't covered under privileged information, apparently. "A boy. He must be ten by now."

I'm hanging on every word, like a dog waiting for a crumb to fall to the floor.

Rachel continues, "Poor Wyatt never got married. Never met anyone, I guess. But ask me, it's because he's still in love with Kerry."

"But she's still married, right?" Marco asks.

Rachel raises her brows. "Think so. How could you divorce someone you can't find?"

True, I think. I already know most of what she's telling me, but maybe there's some small detail or—

"Bet she regrets it all," Rachel goes on. "She dumped a good guy for a serial killer. Her life would have been so different if she'd stayed with Wyatt. Someone secure who could take care of her. But then again, secure might have seemed boring to her. Maybe the killing excited her. Bad boy syndrome taken to the extreme."

I feel myself tense. "I don't think that's the case. She doesn't seem like the type."

Miranda glares at me.

Marco wraps his arm around Rachel. "You're not getting bored with me, are you, darlin'?"

She looks up. "Don't be ridiculous, Marco. But those poor women he killed? I can't even imagine something like that. It makes me sick." She offers a pout to Marco and in return his finger slides over her bottom lip, their minds elsewhere now.

Miranda, still glaring at me, finally speaks again. "Yes, this all makes me sick, too."

Even in the dim lighting, the angry eleven stands out between her eyes like the double l's in the word 'hell,' which is what the rest of the evening is going to be for me. I shrink back in my chair, knowing the subject is closed. Mother's voice, hot and angry, zips through my brain: *You blew it, Adam. Again.*

But Rachel turns from her hubby and drones on, "Anyway, looks like Wyatt might get a second chance with Kerry. Heard they were eating lunch together today."

I sit a little straighter.

"And who knows," she shrugs, "they might have a chance together now. Wyatt's mother recently passed away and—"

"Oh? His mother? That's too bad. I'm so sorry." My heart goes out to him, this man I don't even know, for such a loss.

Miranda huffs.

"Yeah," Rachel agrees. "Anyway, I shouldn't gossip like this, but his mother never liked Kerry. Made that all too clear. Don't know what she'd have done if it weren't for Lucas stealing Kerry away from her Wyatt." She chuckles, takes a quick sip and offers a bit of sage-therapist prophesy: "Probably best that they didn't get together back then. Nothing kills a relationship quicker than a toxic mother-in-law."

I hear a barely audible, "True." But this time I ignore Miranda's jab as my mind whirls. Mrs. Jones had never been interviewed. The mother of an ex-boyfriend of the wife of the killer— only four degrees of separation. Had Lucas *just happened* to land in Joy, *just happened* to persistently go after Kerry, *just happened* to disappear so totally after the crimes leaving Kerry to be separated from Wyatt by years in prison? Had Lucas been bribed, helped? Mother told me often enough, *A mother knows what's best for her kid*. How far would a mother go to protect her son's future?

I look back to Rachel. "So, someone saw the two of them together today?"

"That's right." She nods. "At the casino. Ironically."

"Ironic? How so?"

"That was the last place I saw Kerry, and Lucas, before she went to prison. If you saw the *Strange Murders* episode you know that they—"

"You were there that night?" A pivotal night, with multiple interviews on that episode from bystanders, but not one of my neighbor, who claims she was there, who just might have seen something.

"Yeah, sure was. Got the pictures to prove it."

"Did you know you were going to be working on Kerry Yates's case before we moved here? Is that why you took this job?" Miranda puts the bottle to her lips and tips it back. Marco and Rachel left a half hour ago, but she's still drinking.

"I took this job for you. Because you wanted me to get out of vice, remember? You said it was too dangerous. You hated being a cop's wife, always worrying that I might not come home."

"Yes, but why *here*?" She throws her arms into the air, sloshing wine from the bottle. "Here, in the middle of nowhere?"

My muscles tense. "Don't do this."

She tips back the bottle again, swipes away the residue with the back of her hand. "Do what?"

"Make this all my fault like you always do."

"What's that supposed to mean?"

"You wanted out of the city, away from the traffic, the crowds, the stress. It was your dream to move to a small town and raise a bunch of kids. That's why we bought this massive house, with room to grow. This is your dream, Miranda. Your dream! And I've given up a lot to make it happen."

Her eyes bulge with anger. "Yeah, and I wondered why that was. Why would you give up so much? I thought maybe it was because you love me." She blubbers a bit and then the tears start to flow. "I'm so stupid."

I reach out and gently take the bottle from her hand. My wife is an emotional drunk. "That *is* why I took this job. Because I love you and want to make you happy. All I ever want is for you to be happy."

She jerks away. "I'm not stupid, Adam. You and your mother—"

"Don't make this about my mother."

"How can I not?" Her voice shreds the air. She starts to pace. "Don't you see what this is? You're still grieving her. You need help." She stops and presses her palm to my cheek, as if she cares. It feels cool against my skin. Not just cool, cold. Like the rest of her. How can she be so cruel? My mother has only been gone a couple months.

I start to back away. "Go to bed. You're drunk."

She grabs my arm. "No! You're right." Her eyes grow soft as she continues. "I did push for this," she says. "This isn't your fault. I knew we shouldn't make any decision so soon after her death. What is it they say? No decisions for at least a year."

I frown. It must be the wine. I never win an argument this easily. "What do you mean?"

"Your mother's death. I knew it was hard on you, but I think I've underestimated how hard. It's influencing your decisions now. *Our* decisions apparently."

"No, it's not. I'm fine."

"Come on, Adam. Be honest about this. Those last days when she came to live with us, you remember?"

She always throws this back at me. That she had to leave her part-time job as a teacher's aid and help take care of Mama at home. I never could see the problem; she hated that job anyway. But it remains as staple ammunition for late-night arguments.

"I know it wasn't easy to have her live with us." Appease her, that's always the best way with Miranda. "It's just that I was an only child, and there wasn't anyone else to take care of her."

She leans in closer and rests her head on my shoulder. "I loved having your mother with us in her final days, you know that."

Not true. *All you did was complain.* But I don't say that.

"It's just that every night when you came home after shift, you sat in the family room with her, in front of the television, watching those true crime shows you both liked."

"She was lonely. That's what she liked to watch."

"I know. I know. But don't you see?"

I shake my head, pick up a stack of dirty plates and place them in the sink. The faucet has a ring of lime around it and a steady leak. One more thing to put on the list. Trim hedges. Fix faucet. Make baby. "No, I don't see. What are you getting at?"

She plants herself next to me. "That episode Rachel was talking about, the one with Kerry Yates. Did you watch that with your mother?"

I shrug, keep my guilty face aimed at the faucet as I turn it on, wishing the water would drown out this conversation. "I don't know. Maybe. Why does that matter?"

"You and your mom always bonded over those shows. Watching and solving television crimes together. It was weird, but cute."

"It was one of our favorite things to do together."

She reaches over me and shuts off the water. "Oh, sweetie. This is so hard, isn't it?"

I shrug.

She rubs a circle on my shoulder, leans in closer. "Did you two watch the episode with Kerry Yates close to when your mother passed?"

My eyes dart her way.

"This whole thing is really about your mother's death. That's why you looked for a reason to come here and take this job. You feel like something between you and your mother is still unresolved, and you're here to finish it."

I turn to her, wrap my hand around the small of her back, and pull her close. She's off, way off, but I go along with this explanation. It's a lot better than telling her the real reason I came. Yes, it does have to do with Kerry, but not in the way she thinks. "I married a smart woman."

She grins. "Yes, you did." And she kisses me.

We finish the rest of the bottle of wine in bed, and it finishes us off as well, and I welcome the sound of Miranda's soft snuffling snores before she can ask for more.

It's still dark the next morning when I wake up. I'm chilled but sweaty, lingering in a haze of forbidden images, a strange nightmare still hovering on the edge: *Kerry, naked, splayed on the forest floor, her hair like a dark halo, lips cherry red against white skin and wide open in a silent scream for help. "I'll help you, Kerry." I kneel and caress her cold face, "Shhh shhhh, hush now, I'm here to save you." But I can't. I can't save her because she's already too far gone. "No. No," I cry. "Come back, Kerry. Come back to me." But her limbs stiffen, and her eyes glaze over, and frustration mounts inside me, pulsing through my veins like hot fire, begging to explode. I'm angry, so angry, and I stand and then hack her into a dozen tiny pieces.*

I glance at my phone, 4:00 a.m., and guilt surges through

me, so I reach for Miranda and pull her close. She moans and wiggles her butt close to me, spooning, and placing my hand on her stomach. "Just think, Adam, there could already be a baby started in here."

I move my hand and roll on my side. Admittedly, the thought of a child thrills me. And terrifies me. What if I mess up as a dad? I never knew my father. I'm almost thirty and I should be ready for this phase, but I don't respond.

She turns my way. "So, what did you think of Marco and Rachel last night?" she asks, moving on to a safer topic, away from my silence.

"Liked them. Marco seems great."

"And Rachel?" This is a loaded question. I'm wary.

"I think you two will be good friends. Maybe you should ask her to go shopping or something."

"Would you like it if we were friends?"

"Guess so. If it'd make you happy."

"We made plans to get together for lunch on Friday. She says there's a small café downtown that's good. She offered to introduce me to some of her other friends."

"That's great."

"She's pretty, isn't she?"

"Rachel?" Bad move. Questions are always a way to cover while formulating a pending lie. I knew this because Miranda has told me. She said it was one of the tells she used with her students. "I mean, she's okay. Nothing like you. You're truly beautiful." I lean in and kiss her, just to reiterate my point and have something to do with my mouth besides talk.

Her lips are stiff and cold. I pull back and try to distract by tracing a slow circle over her belly. "Beautiful," I repeat.

Her mouth presses into a grim flat line and my heart rate kicks up a little. I'm doing something wrong, but I have no idea what. Miranda's moods come on like a freight train sometimes, fast and furious, barreling down and taking out anything, sometimes everything, in its path.

I run my hand up her body, over her collarbone and trace my finger along her jawline, weaving it through her hair until I feel her tension ease. Soon her mouth slackens, and her breathing deepens.

Outside, the moon is a full bright disk and the sky bruise-colored over the distant peaks, and once again I'm caught off guard by the landscape. The bedroom window of our Chicago brownstone overlooked a back alley and the "El" tracks. Here we have the gateway to heaven.

I rub and caress and wait, making sure she's fully asleep, and then I swing my legs over the side of the bed. My toe nudges the empty wine bottle and it scutters over the carpet, banks off the corner of the dresser, and spins. I watch, thinking of a childhood game of spin the bottle, where I ended up experiencing my first kiss in a coat closet wedged between a vacuum cleaner and a musty wool coat.

Spin, spin, spin . . . and stop.

The neck of the bottle points to the wall where Miranda has meticulously hung a myriad of family portraits. It's pointing at the photo of my mother.

"Where are you going? It's too early to get up," Miranda says to my back, and I jump as if caught in some dirty act. I clamor into boxers.

"I can't sleep. I thought I'd . . ." I let my voice trail off.

A sigh, and a deep inhale. This one sucks all the air out of the room. "Are you going up to the attic?"

I turn and look down at her, spread out naked over our new emerald green sheets like the forest grass beneath Kerry's naked dead body in my nightmare, and something shifts deep inside me. "I am," I say.

"Don't you think this is getting to be a problem."

"No. Not really."

She huffs and flips over, tucking her knees against her chest and pulling a pillow over her head.

Strange Murders: *"The Hatchet Killer"*
Transcript of the original episode, four years ago

Camera footage of the actress portraying Kerry Yates waiting tables. Host Wesley Steele (voiceover): The White Mountain Café, favorite eating destination for both locals and visitors to the area, and Kerry Grey Yates's place of employment. The Hatchet Killer's second victim, Emily Lynn, was reportedly seen here with her friend several times, even the day she was murdered. Records show that Kerry was working a shift that day, and she waited on the two girls. Could there be a connection between those chance encounters and Emily Lynn's brutal murder? Of course, the café, is one of only two eating establishments in town, so it could be mere coincidence. Or not. It's up to you, the viewers, to decide.

EIGHT

Kerry Grey

My fingers drum the wheel of our 1994 Ford Bronco Tuesday morning, as I pull into a parking space in front of the White Mountain Café. I used to work here, way back when, before parole, before prison, before Lucas left a wake of hacked-up women in my past. I hope to work here again. Or if not here, somewhere. Steady employment is one of the terms of my parole.

Inside, the sign says seat yourself, so I do, snatching a leftover newspaper from next to the counter and sulking into the back booth with the local want ads and a sucky attitude. The breakfast rush has cleared out by now, and it's just me and two gray-haired ladies who sip coffee from rim-kissed mugs. The antithesis of the young duo who sat there four years ago, in their short shorts and crop tops, ready for fun, not a care in the world. I remember a flicker of envy over the dark-haired girl's sexy, ankle-strap, espadrilles. I'd always wanted a pair. I regretted my jealousy later when I heard they found one of her feet with the shoe attached. Now the old ladies glance my way, eyes moving up and down and lips pursing. I squirm and pull the plastic covered menu out from behind the napkin holder. I don't have much money, but I should order something. Eggs or pancakes? I scan the prices. Maybe just a muffin and coffee.

The place has the same red vinyl seats, checkered tablecloths, and brown paneled walls with a neat line of black and white photos: Marilyn, Elvis, James Dean, and the 1998 Joy High School champion football team. Yet everything has changed for me. *Maybe just coffee* . . . that booth by the window is where Lucas sat that night I first met him. Lucas, dark hair and big biceps, the smell of motor grease and a mouth that tasted like hot ash, he—

A glass of water appears in front of me. I look up and see a waitress I've never seen before. I think about asking her if Dani still works here, but she's waiting, pen hovering over her pad. I skim my choices, a small sense of panic taking over, too many choices. Deciding what to eat might seem trivial to most, but after four years of eating what's served, it's an overwhelming task. "Triple berry pie and coffee. Black," I finally say. I replace the menu and go back to the paper, skimming the help-wanted ads. An in-home health care provider or teacher's aid would make in it this town, but I'm neither.

The bell jingles above the door. A heavy, bald man walks in wearing a tight shirt and opens the cash register, taking out a wad of bills and shoving them into his pocket before disappearing through the door that leads to the kitchen. The new boss, I think, and one more strike against a potential job. Mrs. Wojcik must've moved on or passed on. Too bad, she was a nice lady. We had a connection. She'd hire me back, ex-con or not. This guy? Doubtful.

My pie and coffee arrive. I set the paper aside, my focus pulled again toward the gray-haired ladies. They've gone quiet, both staring at the television mounted in the far corner of the room. I wheel around. It's a special news report, and the volume is turned down low. I squint and make out enough of the ticker to see that the lost hiker: Allison Turner, age twenty-three, is still missing. Close to forty-eight hours now. Not good. Even if she is an experienced hiker, the mountains around here are brutal this time of year. It gets down below freezing almost every night. Hypothermia is a big killer in these parts: shivering, numbness, blue lips . . .

I shake off my cold thoughts with a sip of hot coffee. My pie's tasty, purple-blue berries, seedy and sweet. We never had pie in prison. Cake, but never pie. I inhale it, lick the fork clean, and remember that I served Lucas pie that night we met, triple berry pie, and he'd licked the fork clean, running his pointy tongue over the tines while staring at me, giving me a squirmy feeling, deep and hot below my belly, awakening a sense of excitement I didn't know even existed inside me. That's what happens to small town girls like me. We're conditioned early to settle for ordinary and unexciting, and we expect it, even hope for it, the white picket fence dream and all. Back then, before Lucas, my life was destined to be one long line of ordinary. If I could go back, I'd tell my then-self, "Ordinary is good. Boring is good. Wyatt is good." But the way Lucas looked at me that night . . . a tap on my shoulder, and I startle and look up.

A guy, maybe early twenties, stringy muscles and a protruding Adams apple, stands over me, eyes gleaming above a hawkish nose. "Braxton Ryan, Brax. Can I sit down for a sec?"

He takes the seat across from me before I can answer. I push my empty plate aside and fold my arms across my chest and wait.

"President of the Hatchet Club," he says, extending his hand. "Dedicated to finding and bringing Lucas Yates to justice."

I straighten and start to get up from the table.

"Hold on. You'll want to hear what I have to say. It has to do with your husband."

More reason for me to leave. Yet I hesitate.

His lips twitch. "He's still out there. We've spotted him."

"Who's *we*?" A prickle of irritation punctuates my words.

"Club members. About a dozen of us and we have several credible sightings."

"People say that about Sasquatch, too."

"No seriously. There's been an uptick recently. Especially in the woods by your place."

Sunday night, the light in the woods. Lucas? Or this guy? I reach for my mug, but my hand trembles and I can't quite connect the rim to my lips. I set it back down and take a deep breath. Where is that waitress with the check?

"We think you can help us."

"Help you what?"

"Catch Lucas."

"No thank you."

"Come to the next meeting and meet the others. You'll see. They're just normal people like me. Folks who want to see justice served."

Right. Normal like him. A Peeping Tom, his flashlight or lighter in the woods scaring the crap out of me and for what? So his little conspiracy club will have something to talk about over their maps and infrared cameras and—

"You want to get Lucas, right? For what he did to you."

My focus snaps back to the table. "What do you care? Let's be honest. You're not in this for justice. You're in it for the reward money."

"You'd get your share." He nods eagerly as if any amount of money would erase what Lucas has taken from me. "The sheriff's a joke around here. Lucas is practically living in his back yard, and he can't seem to catch him. But you could. With my help."

The waitress plunks my ticket down. I glance at the total, stand, and place a ten-dollar bill on it. That's a four-dollar tip, more than I can afford, but I've got to get out of here, away from this conversation.

He follows me, still talking. "The reward money is up to a hundred grand."

I pass the gray-haired ladies' table. They're watching intently.

"I'd think you would at least want to find Lucas to clear your name," he says. "If not for you, then maybe for your son."

I turn, snap, "Leave my son out of this."

"Fine. But some people think that you coming back here is why that girl is missing."

"I don't know anything about that."

"I'm not saying you do. Got to admit, though, it's a weird coincidence. I'm thinking you being here has . . . uhm . . . reactivated Lucas."

He follows me onto the sidewalk. I'm not sure how to shake this guy. "None of this has anything to do with me. I'm trying to get my life back on track. Get things figured out."

"I know. I know. I get it. And the reward money could help with that. Come to the next meeting. Work with us. You won't regret it. You may come to find that you need our help."

"What in the world for?"

He shrugs. "History has a way of repeating itself."

"I'm never going back to prison again, if that's what you're thinking."

"I hope not. I'd hate to see you take the fall for another crime. And that wouldn't happen if Lucas was behind bars where he belongs. We could help you with that."

Give it up, buddy. I sidestep him and jerk the car door open. "The answer is no."

His shifts his focus from me to the the inside of my Bronco. His mouth drops just a bit as his eyes widen.

I follow his gaze to the passenger side seat . . . and a hatchet.

Strange Murders: *"The Hatchet Killer"*
Transcript of the original episode, four years ago

Interview with Sheila Berg, MD, FAPA, Lewis County Mental Health Center: Sheriff Foley consulted me regarding this case. We explored the possibility of the alleged killer being addicted to some sort of narcotic, specifically a stimulant, due to the sheer strength and extraordinary stamina it would take to disassemble a body with a hatchet. A stimulant such as meth, or meth mixed with an opioid, known as speed-balling, could provide the type of energy that would have been needed to perpetrate this crime. Serial killers experience a high after taking the life of their victim, much like an addict after a hit. When the killer can't relieve his cravings for killing, he'll often turn to the high he receives from an illicit narcotic. My conclusions pointed to a high probability that the Hatchet Killer regularly abused illegal narcotics or was a full-blown addict. Sheriff Foley hoped that the killer's need for a fix might draw him out of hiding.

NINE

Adam Nash

Indian Creek Road runs north of town adjacent to the county landfill. I make two passes before spying the mobile home parked at the back of the lot. I continue rolling down the road, pull off and park. Kerry isn't my only parolee, I've got a full case load, including other guys like this one, Ty Hendricks, who served three years of a five-year narcotic possession sentence, paroled early, but hasn't shown for his last three mandated appointments.

Hendricks doesn't have a history of violence, but I've heard horror stories about parole home visits. Officers getting shot, stabbed, worse . . . I pop the guard on my holster and crouch low, pushing through the weeds. The place is a junkyard. Coils of barbwire, an old bed frame, and a late model Seville with the hood up, rusted and void of glass. Behind the trailer sets a large metal building, green and white, with an arched roof and a double wide door. Hendricks's red Chevy truck is parked in front of it.

I'm closer to the mobile home now and my nose twitches at the smell of weed seeping through the cracks in the siding. There's a satellite attached to the roof, tattered curtains cover a large front window, and the screen door hangs by one hinge. Hendricks could stand to do some work around the place.

I reach the front steps and the sound of gunfire startles me, then I breathe again as the cries of fallen zombies echo from inside the trailer. I bang on the door and step to the side, my hand hovering over my gun. Inside, the video game goes silent, and the curtain in the front window parts. After some scuffling noises, the door cracks open. A head pops out and swivels like an owl.

I step out and identify myself.

His slitty eyes go wide. He slips back inside, slams the door, and clicks the deadbolt.

I bang on the door again. "County Parole! Open up now!"

The noises grow louder. What's the guy trying to do? Run? Hide? I pull my cell, about to call for backup, when I hear a gurgling noise, then the sound of furniture moving and something else. What? My senses kick into high alert. Self-harm? "Hendricks? What's going on in there, buddy? We just need to talk, that's all."

The only sound is the distant rattling of semi-trucks along the highway.

"I'm here to help you, Hendricks. Let's talk about this, okay?"

Again, no response. I move to the back of the trailer and find the door ajar. A quick scan of the yard, but no sign of Hendricks. My skin prickles. *What's going on here?* "Hendricks? You in there? Hey, man, I just want to get you some help. That's all."

I enter the trailer, my weapon poised low as I swim through a cloud of weed smoke. It's dark, dank, and there's junk everywhere; soiled clothing, empty beer cans, pizza boxes, greasy take-out bags. This guy lives like a cockroach. I pass through the living room, clear, into the kitchen, clear, down a short hallway to the bedroom, clear, and . . . a toilet flushes—he's ditching drugs—I backtrack to the hallway just in time to see him slip out the back door.

I follow, searching the backyard and finally spotting him

slinking into the rusty metal outbuilding at the back of the lot. I run after him, sweat dripping down my face as I squeeze through the outbuilding door. Inside, my eyes strain to adjust to the darkness, piles of tires, an old riding mower, uncoiled chicken wire . . . a hollow ping reverberates off the metal wall behind me.

I raise my gun and spin. "Give it up, Hendricks. This isn't going to do you any good. You're only pissing me off."

A shuffling sound to my right, and I whirl, pointing my gun. Nothing. *Where are you, you crazy SOB?*

Then I hear the distinct sound of a door sliding shut. A bolt slides and locks and a chain rattles as it's secured. High-pitched laughter moves around the outside walls of the building. I trace its path through the darkness and . . . oh no. I start moving, outstretched arms groping through the shadows toward a small door at the back of the building, move . . . move—aaah!—my knee rams something . . . hot pain shoots through my thigh . . . keep going, move faster . . . but the back door rattles as it scrapes rocky ground . . . I lunge forward and throw my body into the door, crashing against the metal, but the *clink* of steel seals my fate. The door won't budge.

Outside, the sound of pounding footsteps fades into the distance, a car door slams shut, and an engine roars to life. The walls close around me along with the smell of dusty metal and grease and gasoline. I sink to the ground, rubbing my sore knee. So much for being a big city Chicago ex-cop. Welcome to the boondocks.

I put in a call to Amber. "Send Bird or McCulley to Hendricks's place. I'm okay but he's locked me in one of the outbuildings. Tell them they'll need bolt cutters."

"Will do," she says earnestly. But before she hangs up, her throaty giggle fills my ear. So does the echo of Mother's voice: *You screwed up, boy.*

Strange Murders: *"The Hatchet Killer"*
Transcript of the original episode, four years ago

Interview with Chet Hanson, Lewis County Deputy Coroner:
I was on the team that conducted the dismemberment investi-
gation. It was the most complicated postmortem investigation
I've encountered in my career, but after a lengthy process, we
were able to distinguish a pattern of disarticulation. (Picks up
a hatchet) You see, when a harder material, like the steel of a
blade, makes contact with a softer substance, such as bone,
it leaves a toolmark. We call them kerf marks. In the case of
that first victim, the bones consistently showed V-shaped kerf
marks with macroscopic and microscopic impact fractures
consistent with an axe or hatchet. Considering the type of tool
used, it would have taken a considerable amount of time and
strength to dismember the body. Often when we see dismem-
berment, it's been used to conceal the identity of the victim,
or evidence of a crime, but in this case, the killer left the body
parts to be discovered, even staged the dismembered leg by the
head of the trail. It would be like butchering an animal, not a
human, and displaying a trophy. It shows a complete detach-
ment from the victim's humanity. That's when I knew that this
was one sick killer.

TEN

Kerry Grey

I drive through town thinking about the hatchet. It bothers me. It must belong to Pops, but I don't remember it on the way to school this morning. Wouldn't Joey have said something about it? *Did someone put the hatchet in the Bronco while I was in the café?*

Paranoia creeps over me as I turn onto 9th Street and pull into the school parking lot. My gaze darts to my rearview mirror, then back to the lot where I spot a woman leaning against a sleek black Mercedes and watching me drive by. As soon as I park, she makes a beeline for my Bronco. I quickly shove the hatchet under the passenger seat. She taps on my window.

I crank it open and she asks, "You're Joey's mom, right?"

"Right."

"I'm Trish. Aiden's mother."

She's red-haired and freckled, dressed in a pink sundress. A sweet little thing, like a little pack of sugar. In prison, someone would tear her open and gobble her up. I can't imagine what she wants from me. Don't want to know. I sigh and look past her to the crowd of kids emerging from the school, hoping that Joey's on his way.

"Our boys are in the same class," she explains.

My muscles tense. "That's great."

Her eyes flatten. "Yesterday Aiden came home and told me something strange."

"Oh yeah."

"Yes. He said that Joey had brought a small carved bird to school."

"Bird . . .?"

"That's right. Carved from bone."

Anxiety squirms deep in my stomach.

"He told Aiden that it was animal bone."

I exhale.

"Joey said that his father had carved the bird for him."

"Really?" I don't remember Lucas carving anything for Joey back then. Maybe, but that was a long time ago. "I don't understand," I say. "Is there a problem?"

"His *father* carved it?" She looks at me like I'm an idiot.

And then it hits me. "You mean like—"

"Recently."

I swallow hard. "That can't be right. Joey must have meant that Lucas carved it for him a long time ago."

"That's not what he told Aiden. He said that it was a new and a gift from his dad."

"Well, you know kids. They make up stuff all the time . . ." I see Joey wandering between parked cars looking for me. I tap the horn and wave him over. "Hey sweetie." He climbs inside and I crank the engine, shooting Trish a sweet smile. "It's been good talking to you. Take care."

We're not even out of the lot before Joey starts in, "Don't call me sweetie in front of other people, okay?"

"Okay."

"You know Aiden's mom?"

"Just met her."

"Really? Why'd you meet her?"

"She introduced herself."

"You mean, like she wants to be your friend?"

"Maybe. Would it be weird if I became friends with some of the other mothers at school?"

He shrugs. "No. Guess not."

"Are you friends with Aiden?"

"Sort of. We talk sometimes."

"You should have him come by. You know, to hang out."

"I don't think so." He turns on the radio and shrinks into the seat, pulling his hat down low. My fifteen seconds of allotted conversation time is over. The bird thing is a problem, but it'll have to wait until later. Preferably when Pops is with me. He knows Joey better than me now. Four years of once-a-month, sterile, rule-laden, supervised prison visits did nothing for Joey and me, except chip away at our relationship. He's growing up, no longer my little boy, his baby fat is gone and his face angular, a kid I barely know, can only hope to get to know again, if I could just get him to talk to me beyond a few forced seconds.

We ride the rest of the way in silence, me steeling glances Joey's way. There's a lot of his father in him, I spied that already, and it worries me because history repeats itself. At least that's what I've been told. And believe. Because for me, the damage began the moment I was born, or so I'd learned one day when I was seven and hiding under the church hall table listening to the old men jawing away about town folk. Didn't expect to hear my own mother's name, but there it was, loud and clear, Mora Grey, the poor thing, too young to be expecting a child and not even properly married. Old Doc Lou was there. He said that my mother was just sixteen when he slit her belly open and pulled me out, slimy pink, writhing and squealing like a new piglet. A sad thing it was, he said, she'd only held me for a minute before the bleed-out started. He couldn't get it to stop, and she oozed from her cut until her body dried up like rain fallen on August asphalt.

The rest of the story I already knew. My father, whoever he was, split—*too young, too young*—and Pops did the best he could, widowed already and working odd jobs until he saved enough to buy a five-acre patch of scrub and dirt on the mountain, where he eked out a living as a woodworker, and prided himself on being self-reliant. "Don't depend on nobody but God and yourself," he always told me. Words that got me through prison alive, and back to my son. Now if I could only figure out how to fix our relationship.

We reach the cabin and Pops is waiting for us on the porch. Joey walks past him, the screen door slamming behind him.

"Something wrong with that boy?"

"Like I'd know. He doesn't ever talk to me."

"Hmm." He pushes out of the rocking chair. I see him wince.

"What is it, Pops?"

"Old bones, that's all. Glad you're back with the Bronco. I got to get it loaded and run an order down to Pete's Corner before the sun sets."

"I'll help," I say, and we work on it together, like old times. I'd done this through my childhood, chopping and bundling wood for sale. Pops's regular customers are his bread and butter, those folks who heat their homes mainly with wood. Still common in this area where lots of folks live primitively. Campers bring in money, too. Not as steady, though. It's hard work, real work, and it's sucking the juice right out of Pops.

We're almost done loading the wood when I bring up what happened at school. "This mom stopped me after school. She said that Joey brought in a bird carved out of bone."

"Like antler, you mean?" He shuts the tailgate.

"Maybe. But Joey told the kids that Lucas carved it. And not a long time ago, like you'd think, but recently." I let it hang there, waiting to see what he says.

"Kids say all sorts of things that aren't true to get attention and whatnot. Wouldn't worry about it."

"Then there's no chance that Joey saw Lucas while I was in prison?"

"Don't you think I'd know if he did?"

"Yeah. Sure. I'm just asking. Do you think you could talk to him about it? Maybe ask why he'd be showing it around?"

"No. That's your job."

Like I'll get anywhere with him. We're finished with the load and it's ready to go. My arms feel like rubber. "Hey, did you leave one of your hatchets in the Bronco? Gave someone a good scare. Should have seen the look on this guy's face when he saw it."

He scowls. "No. Don't think so. What hatchet?"

I go around to the passenger side and pull it out from under the seat. "This one."

Pops stares at it a long time. "Don't know where that came from, but it's not mine."

Strange Murders: *"The Hatchet Killer"*
Transcript of the original episode, four years ago

Interview with Steve Green, Kootenai Forest Ranger: As soon as we were notified that Yates was on the run in the forest, we sent out choppers and ground search units. We worked in full cooperation with local and state authorities. There must have been a few hundred people, including deputy reserves, involved in a weeklong search for Lucas Yates. There was no trace of the man. Since then, we've had several folks claim to have seen Yates, but this is rough country. Not many men could survive out here for the long term. Ask me, he's either bear food or he crossed into Canada.

ELEVEN

Adam Nash

I pass the time locked in Hendrick's metal building scrolling through The Hatchet Club's website on my phone and thinking about the bloody mannequin leg. Foley thought it was these people taking things too far. They are organized, I'll give them that. They've got a list of Lucas Yates sightings, including an interactive map with dropped pins at each set of coordinates. The most recent sighting was a couple days ago near a branch of the Tobacco River, about five miles out of town and less than a mile from where Kerry lives.

I read the report: *I spotted a large man, who I believe to be Lucas Yates, on the shore of the Tobacco River. He had dark hair and a long beard. He wore jeans and what looked to be a shirt made of animal skin. He was bent over, drawing water from the river. I approached, calling his name, and he slipped back into the woods. I searched the area, but he'd simply vanished like a ghost. Report number #12, by R.S., April 12.*

R.S. is a probably some nutcase, trumping up a fake sighting for attention, I tell myself, but my jaw clenches at the idea of someone capturing Yates before me.

Amateurs, Mama says. *Don't let them get ahead of you, boy.*

I'm trying, Mama. I'm trying.

Another report, this one from last August and it makes my skin crawl: *I was camping at Beartrap Canyon and overlooked an open area that butted up to the woods. I saw a dark form that stood upright and looked like a person. Retrieving my binoculars, I scanned the area, but the person was gone. I investigated the area where he had stood and found human tracks. I followed the tracks for about ten minutes through an area that was mostly wooded with some open spots of short field type grass and dirt. The trail was difficult to follow, and I was afraid of getting lost, so I turned back. When I got back to my campsite, I found that the man had doubled back and was rifling through my belongings. I yelled and started to run after him, when I recognized his face and eagle tattoo on his bicep. It was Lucas Yates. He was lean and wild looking. Scared the crap out of me, and I told him to take what he needed. He took a couple packages of food and left. I packed up camp and got out of there. I'm a believer now. The Hatchet Killer is still out there. I saw him with my own eyes. Report number #08, by T.W., August 4.*

I continue reading sightings until the clanking of metal draws my attention away from my screen. A few seconds later, the lock drops with a *clunk*. The door opens and Amber stands there, bolt cutters in hand, chomping on gum.

"Where are McCulley and Bird?" I ask.

"Busy with the hiker. It's just me."

"I've been waiting over an hour. What took you so long?"

"I have other things to do besides take care of you, you know." She gives me a once over. "Thought you'd know better anyway. A big city cop with so much experience and everything."

"What?"

"I said, I thought you'd know—"

"I heard you. Let's get out of here. There's something else I need your help with."

"It's after five. Work's done." She snaps her gum. "And maybe I've got plans."

"This isn't really work-related. It's something personal."

Her lips curve into a slow smile.

Strange Murders: *"The Hatchet Killer"*
Transcript of the original episode, four years ago

Interview with Bob Kenny, owner of The Gold Bar Casino (continued), Joy, Montana: Everyone in town eventually comes through my bar. Lucas Yates was no exception. Mostly he came in with his work buddies, usually around payday to blow off some steam, you know, do a little drinking, flirt with the tourist girls. The usual stuff. He wasn't a drunk, I mean I don't serve drunks, and I eighty-six anyone looking for a fight, let 'em take it outside. I run a friendly watering hole overall. Nah, Lucas never caused any trouble. He seemed like an okay guy back then. But you never really know, do you?

TWELVE

Adam Nash

"That's your third drink in less than a half hour," Amber says as she eyes my almost empty glass. We're at The Gold Bar, in a booth under the red glow of a neon Budweiser sign.

I ignore her and continue drinking, doodling on a napkin, my mind somewhere else.

"Is this that *personal* thing you needed me for? Because I don't normally do the designated driver thing."

"No, this isn't it. Just needed a few drinks to take the edge off, that's all."

"Oh, then you do have something else in mind?" She reaches across the table, her hand connecting with mine. "Care to tell me what it is? I'm here for you. For whatever you need."

My gaze roams from her spidery lashes to her moist, pink lips, slightly open, her soft tongue lingering, down the line of her neck to the soft indent of her throat and lower, back to the curve of her breasts, swelling with each breath, Liberty's wings rhythmically flapping.

I've sunk to a new low. My voice of reason, Mama's voice, always dissipates with liquor, but she obviously disapproves of my behavior and remains audible, a low monotonous humdrum, like the fan humming from the corner of the bar—

whrrr, click, whrrr, click, you're a prick, you're a . . . "Stop it."

Amber jerks back and withdraws her hand. "Sorry. I thought we were on the same page."

"Not you. I didn't mean you." I lick my lower lip. "I do need something. And I need it badly."

Her hand is back again. "Yes . . .?"

"A tattoo."

I stumble across the threshold of Pony's Ink Shop, a converted garage off Highway 93, and into a haze of clove-smelling smoke. Amber rushes past me and into the arms of a short, skinny guy, baseball cap backward over longish black hair. I get caught up in looking at his tats, my gaze stuck on the snake winding around the left side of his neck.

Amber breaks from the hug and runs her hand over my shoulder. "Adam, this is Pony. You're in good hands with him. He's a master."

Alternative rock thuds through mounted corner speakers at about the same tempo as my heartrate. I blink as much from the smoke haze as from realizing where I am and what I'm doing. Amber likewise blinks, then tilts back her head and squeezes a couple drops into her eyes. Pony's dark eyes survey my khakis and button down. His lip curls. "What are you looking for, Adam?"

"A tattoo."

"I get that. What type?"

Amber swipes her fingernail over her chest. "He's been admiring Liberty."

Pony nods. "Some of my best work. You want something like that?"

"Yeah. Yeah, I do. Maybe with a slight modification."

His brows shoot up. "Modification? Something there you don't like?"

I snap my gaze from Amber's cleavage. "No, that's not it. I want to personalize it, that's all." I hand over the folded napkin from my front shirt pocket.

He looks at my design. "Interesting. Come on over." He points to a what looks like a dentist's chair covered in plastic. "Have a seat." He scoots next to me in a wheeled stool, a clipboard balanced on his knee while he sketches my design onto a sheet of paper. "You been self-medicating?"

"What do you mean?"

"I detect whiskey."

"A little," Amber tells him. "Don't be too hard on him. He's a virgin."

"A what?" I shoot Pony a knowing look and chuckle. "Hardly."

He smirks, tosses aside his pencil and shows me the paper. "How's this?"

I nod as my spirts lift. Then fall as he starts to prep the station, needles, a gun-like thing covered with plastic . . . "Where do you want it?"

"The same place Lucas Yates got his."

He hesitates, fingers a big button-type-thing stretching his earlobe, then lets out a long sigh. "Fine. Take off your shirt."

I start to unbutton. "Is something wrong?"

He clicks an armrest into place. "I don't get the fascination with the guy, that's all. He's a killer."

I pull off my shirt, self-conscious of the pit stains on my T-shirt. "You do a lot of these then?"

"At least one a week."

"Mine's unique, though, right?"

"Yeah. Definitely. T-shirt, too."

I take off my T-shirt, avoiding my reflection in the mirror, feeling the heat of Amber's gaze on my bare flesh.

"You part of that club in town?" Pony asks.

"No. Why?"

"Because they all want Yates's tat. Like it makes them one with him or something."

I shift in the chair. The plastic crackles under my skin. "Amber's got one like it."

"Uh, huh. What's the deal? You and her a thing? 'Cuz you don't look like her type." He gives her a wink and she giggles.

"No. We just work together."

"Gotcha." He now holds a patch of gauze soaked in alcohol, motions for my arm.

"I like the music playing in here. What is it?"

"The Verve. Older stuff."

"It's good." It's making my head hurt. Or maybe it's the smell in here.

"Yeah? Glad you approve." He motions for my arm again. I notice that each one of his fingers has a letter inked on the knuckle. I point at his hand. "What's that spell?"

He stops, clenches his fists and puts his hands together: LOVE PAIN. "Enough stalling, put your arm up here." He swings a light overhead. It casts weird shadows over his face, turning his features demon-like, fitting since I'm about to be carved with the mark of the beast.

He swipes my skin clean with the antiseptic. I brace myself. "Why'd Yates pick the eagle? Do you know?"

"Yates again?"

"Yeah."

"You got a lot of questions about him." He snaps on gloves and picks up the pen.

The first needle prick sends a shiver of pain straight through to my bone.

I try to ignore it and concentrate on what I'm here for: answers. I prod Pony by listing specific possibilities, like I was trained to do in interrogations. "The eagle means different things to different people," I say. "Power. Spiritual heights. Hunter."

His gaze briefly slides my way. "Hunter?"

"The eagle carries its prey, right?" Again and again the needle pierces my skin, like tiny, sharp talons scratching at my arm until the stings blend into a single hot burn.

"I don't know what it meant to Yates. Could've been anything. We didn't discuss it."

"Amber says you inked him right before he went on his killing spree."

"Coincidence."

"Not saying it wasn't. Just wondering about his mindset. One day getting a tattoo, the next day . . ."

"He seemed completely normal. Sort of like you."

"Like me?"

"Yates wasn't really into getting inked."

"I'm into it."

"You're into it because she's into it. And you want to get into—"

"Yates was getting a tattoo to impress his wife?"

"No guy does this to impress his wife. Is your wife going to be impressed?" He leans back with a half grin, knowing the answer, and swipes with the antiseptic again.

I glance over at Amber. She winks.

"Who was Yates trying to impress?" I ask Pony.

"You tell me, man." He shrugs and bends back over my arm. The needle pricks black ink along my skin while Mama's voice pricks at my brain. *You got a lead, boy. Good job.*

Strange Murders: *"The Hatchet Killer"*
Transcript of the original episode, four years ago

Interview Evelyn Brodie, mother of Hatchet Killer victim Samantha Brodie: Sam had just finished nursing school. She'd worked hard and wanted a break. She made plans with two other nursing students to head to Joy for a long weekend of backpacking and rafting. Just the girls. I talked to her that morning, a quick hello. She sounded tired, hungover maybe, and was eating breakfast at the diner. She told me she'd partied with some locals the night before. I think that's when she must have met Lucas Yates. That was the last time I ever talked to my baby . . .

THIRTEEN

Kerry Grey

I sit back, close my eyes, and reacquaint myself with the sounds of my childhood. It's after supper, and Pops is cleaning up the kitchen, Joey's gone to his bed, and I've settled in the rocking chair on the front porch, a wool throw wrapped over my shoulders. Spring is late this year, snow caps still retreating, and the mountain's runoff ripples and burbles through our creek. In the distance, coyotes yip and the tree frogs croak, working themselves into a frenzied crescendo.

My hand falls to Boone curled next to my chair, and I find a dash of comfort in the familiar feel of his fur, but then a shiver crawls over me and I pull the blanket tighter around my shoulders and start to rock. An unsettled feeling overwhelms me. Maybe it's that hatchet that showed up without explanation, or the bone carving, or . . . who knows? Something has set my nerves on edge. Nothing I can pinpoint, exactly, just a growing unease inside me. I rock in a slow rhythmic back and forth, hoping to calm my nerves. I stare hard into the night as if the answers to all my problems are written in the cool mountain air like white chalk on a blackboard. If only it could be that easy.

After a while, Pops turns off the main light. I rock a while longer, the *creech, creech* of the rocker soothing me. I tuck my chin into the blanket, protecting my face from the buzzing mosquitos and my mind wanders to time in woods as a young girl. I was famous even before I married a serial killer. At least in these parts. Every year in the fall, at the close of hunting season, Joy celebrated a festival called Buck Days. The Legion had its annual flapjack breakfast, a small carnival for kids in the Casino's parking lot, a street dance with a live band and beer tent, and the Big Buck contest. A thousand dollars for the largest rack. Imagine the talk when a nine-year-old girl took the purse. Especially when it came out that I'd field dressed the animal myself. The men competing for that prize money could excuse a youngster's lucky shot, but it was a flagrant slap in their male ego that a task like gutting the kill could be carried out by a girl. And years later, when body parts piled up and I was arrested? Most of those men hadn't forgotten their lost prize, and public opinion tried me as sure as any jury.

I quit rocking, let the night's sounds wrap around me, and wonder, if I'd been a boy would—a sharp cracking sound startles me. I jerk upright and stare hard at the trees. The breeze dies down, so do the frogs' night calls, and a chill comes over me as the silence settles like a wet blanket. Boone snores softly, oblivious or unconcerned by the sounds. Then more popping, the sound of a twig breaking, and a shadow moves in the trees, barely noticeable under the faint hint of moonlight. I watch as it moves from tree to tree, and then fades deep into the woods. The lost hiker? No, she'd come to the cabin for help. That weird Hatchet Club guy I'd met at the café? Fear kicks up as I think of that flicker of light the other night. Or Lucas? Is he out there right now? I shake it off. Impossible, I think. Pops is right. That light was nothing more than the moon reflecting off a coyote's eyes. Or a coydog. We'd had trouble with them before. Why am I so jumpy? How many times had I seen shadows at the forest's edge? Deer, elk, bear . . . the Kootenai comes to life at night. No matter what that Hatchet Club guy says, or the crazy lady at the casino, Lucas is long gone. He'd be stupid to hang around here.

The screen door creeks open and Pops steps onto the porch. "You going to stay out here all night?"

"Just a while longer."

"Okay. I'm heading to bed."

"Goodnight, Pops."

Boone's barking wakes me from a deep sleep. It's 2:00 a.m. and I slip jeans under my T-shirt, slide into my shoes, and meet Pops in the kitchen. He's wearing a T-shirt and cargo pants, his fly unzipped with striped boxers showing through, and his knuckles white-gripped around the stock of a 12-gauge shotgun. "Go back to bed. Something's after the hens. I'll take care of it."

Joey peeks over the edge of the loft.

I shake my finger at him. "Get back in bed and stay there. You understand?"

I listen for his door to shut, and I turn back. Pops is already outside on the porch. "Wait, wait. I saw something in the trees earlier."

He pauses and looks over his shoulder. "Like what?"

"I don't know, but something bigger than a coon."

He continues walking. I pull a flashlight from the kitchen cabinet and catch up to him in the front yard.

The cool night air slaps my skin, and the grass is heavy with night dew, and Boone is eerily quiet now. The hen house looks still and dark. We open the door and shine the light over a dozen or more roosted hens, feathers fluffed and beaks tucked. A couple unwind and look our way, the flashlight beam turning their eyes into glassy little beads.

A breeze kicks up, leaves rustle, and a sound like a woman's long mournful cry cuts the night air. We both turn to see the barn door swinging open on rusty hinges. Pops grips the shotgun tighter and starts that way.

Inside the barn, dust floats on moonbeams, while odors of the moldy straw, animal waste, and hog sweat fill the air. The sow grunts from her pen in the back of the barn, and there's the slight sound of scurrying—a mouse, gorging on spilt feed grain. The light beam glints off the steel of Pop's tools: hammers and saws, hatchets and axes, planers and carvers, all of them lined up like soldiers on the battlefield, ready for whatever job needs to be done.

"There's nothing out here," I say.

"Someone was out here. I locked this door. I always do."

I skim the flashlight beam over the ground, looking for tracks or footprints. "I don't see anything. Let's head back inside. It's a couple hours until daybreak. We can come back out and take another look then."

Pops nods and we head back to the house. As I trudge upstairs, something seems off. For a second, I can't place it, then I do. Joey's door is open. He'd shut it before I went outside with Pops.

"Joey?" I flip on the light. "Jo—Joey!"

Under the bed? *No.* My heart sinks. Inside the closet? *No.*

I stand in the middle of the room, my world spinning, my breath caught in my throat. Distraction, I think. The barn was a distraction to get us out of the house so someone could get at Joey.

My baby, my baby, my baby . . .

"Kerry?" Pops is behind me, his face a mask of confusion. "What's wrong?"

"He's gone. Joey's gone." I push past him and run down stairs, out the door, and across the yard to the treehouse— empty!—and back to the cabin.

"He's not there," I tell Pops.

A low guttural sound escapes his lips as he grabs a couple

of lanterns, throws on a coat, fills a canteen . . . I do the same, and he hands me one of the lanterns and pockets a full box of shotgun shells.

We pick up tracks at the edge of the woods, two clear sets of prints: a man's boot and Joey's sneaker prints. He'd showed me his new sneakers my first day back, he was so proud of them. Pops had sold a piece of furniture, had extra money, took the kid into Libby, and bought him a good pair of shoes, a brand name. He really wanted them, Pops had said, all the kids at school have that type. It seemed to be a big deal to Joey.

Of course, it was. What ten-year-old wants to wear shoes from the grocery store?

I should have been here all these years, working and getting him the things he needs. I'm a screw up of a mother.

"Over here." Pops points his beam along the forest floor. The prints move along a game trail. I take the lead, my hand clenching the lantern, as I half-run through the woods. Pops breath comes hard and steady behind me. We're moving downhill now, my feet catching on tree roots and fallen branches. I pitch forward, catch myself, and keep going. A minute later I stop and shine my light around. We've reached the river. There's no sign that anyone has been here.

"What now?" My voice is thin. Which way do we go? "We have to split up."

"No, Kerry. We have to stay together. What if—"

"No way. We'll lose too much time. Once he gets deeper into these woods, he'll disappear." My blood surges. My voice shrill with panic. "Just do as I say. Please. Go that way."

I go left, pushing my way through the trees, my nostrils burn with the smell of pine, and sap sticks to my hair. Shadows dance in my peripheral vision, tears stream down my face . . . there's too much space to cover, he could be anywhere. I'm losing hope when I hear the distant sound of a shotgun.

Pops! A signal. I spin, orientate myself to the sound, and start running, my feet pounding the ground until I reach our initial spot. I stop. I'm confused. *Where are they?*

Crack!—another shot and I'm running again, and screaming, "Pops! Joey!"

"Over here. Over here!" *He found him! Oh God, please let him be okay.* Another shot and I jerk toward the sound and burst into a clearing. Before me stands Pops, his gun pointed to the sky. He lowers it and smiles. Joey is next to him.

I drop to my knees. "Thank you, thank you, thank you." My body trembles as I stretch out my arms. "Joey."

But he doesn't come to me. Instead, he glares with eyes full of hate. "You scared him away."

I drop my arms. "What? Who?"

"My dad."

Strange Murders: *"The Hatchet Killer"*
Transcript of the original episode, four years ago

Interview with Sheriff Foley: We recovered surveillance video from the night of the disappearance of the Hatchet Killer's third victim, Emily Lynn, showing her exiting The Gold Bar at approximately 1:30 a.m. She appeared to be following and talking to an unidentifiable person, who walked out of the range of the surveillance camera. Was this person the Hatchet Killer? If so, it appears that the person knew the exact limitations of the bar's surveillance camera. We investigated this lead thoroughly, questioning bar employees and the company that installed the camera, but we hit a brick wall.

FOURTEEN

Kerry Grey

It is another quiet ride to school on Wednesday morning. Joey sits with his arms crossed, staring forward and bottled up tight. He's still angry with me, and I have no idea how to talk to him about his father, or anything else. Under my seat is a small box I found hidden in his treehouse, and inside are several carved effigies, including the small bird Aiden's mother had mentioned, and a hand-carved bone knife. Something else, too, that I'd kept in my pocket. "We're going to have to talk about last night."

He turns and looks out the window.

"I told you to stay in your room. What made you go outside?"

He shakes off my question.

"Answer me, Joey."

"I wanted to see Dad, okay?"

"But you didn't *see* him, did you?"

"He was there. I know he was."

"What makes you so sure it was your dad?" I'd seen the footprints and knew someone was there, but was it Lucas lurking in the woods? Or someone else? I don't know which is more terrifying.

Joey's fingers work over the strap on his backpack. The tension in the Bronco grows heavier.

"You've been waiting for him, haven't you?"

He nods.

"Because he brings you gifts."

He rotates in his seat, his body tense and fist clenched. "You were in my treehouse."

My hands shake. I grip the steering wheel tighter. The school is up ahead.

"You found my things!"

"Are they from your father?"

"That's none of your business. They're mine! Where are they?"

"Tell me how you got them."

"He leaves them for me in my treehouse."

"You see him leave them?"

"No. I just find them, okay? Where are they? What have you done with them?"

"Please calm down."

"I can't believe you took my things!" He pops open the door and starts to slide out.

I slam on the breaks and crank the wheel, screeching to a stop on the curb. A horn blast slices the air as the person behind me swerves to avoid hitting us. "Joey! What are you—?"

"I hate you!" he screams and slams the door.

My chest tightens, and my throat constricts with anxiety. I collapse forward, my forehead on the steering wheel, trying to catch my breath. Lucas isn't dead. He's not escaped across the border and living incognito in Canada. He's been here the whole time, in our own back yard, leaving gifts for our son. Gifts carved out of bone.

I'd always felt out of place at Wyatt's home, like an old piece of furniture that someone was going to discard at any moment. I feel that way early this morning as I seek Wyatt's advice. I dropped off Joey and came directly here, and now we sit beneath a soaring cathedral-like ceiling, on buttery calf-skinned sofas, sipping coffee in front an enormous wall of windows and a sweeping view of the surrounding mountains. All of it makes me feel small.

I'd thought of this house many times when I lived with Lucas, wondering what it would have been like had I somehow ended up with Wyatt, living here. Not that I was unhappy in my marriage. At least not at first. The old saying, money doesn't buy happiness, is true. Lucas and I were poor, but happy, and we were rich in other things, our love, Joey, our tiny little home. Sure, Lucas drank a little too much and would sometimes disappear for a few days on an alcohol binge, but . . .

I set a knife on the table.

Wyatt picks it up. "What's this?"

"It's Joey's."

He runs his fingers along the smooth handle, up to the hilt and then along the razor-sharp blade, knapped out of flint. "Primitive. Well made. Whoever did this has some skill." He looks up. "Where'd you get this?"

"It's Joey's."

"He made this?"

"No. Lucas."

He sets it down, clasps his fingers together, and swallows hard. "Lucas?"

I tell him about the night before, the scare in the woods, the other mothers at school and what Aiden's mom had said about the carved bird, and Joey's words this morning, and then I put it all together for him. "Lucas is still in the area. I think he comes down and visits Joey and brings him gifts." I point at the knife. "Gifts like this. And that bird. All this stuff was hidden in the treehouse."

"Are you absolutely sure? Did Joey say these were from Lucas?"

"No, but—"

"Could be that one of his friends made these. Or Pops? Did you check with him?"

"Pops didn't make them. Joey showed the carved bird to a friend at school and told him they were gifts from his father." I feel a tremor kick up deep inside me. I try to quell it, but it's spreading, growing, and taking over. I want to fold in on myself, ball up, like I'd done so many nights in prison on my bunk in the dark. But this is different. I'm not alone and it's not dark. I breathe deeper and will my body to calm. "Lucas has been watching from the woods," I say through chattering teeth. "Watching Joey's window. There's more, too." I tell him about the hatchet in the Bronco. "A warning," I say. "He wants Joey and . . . and I'm going to be his next victim."

"No." Wyatt shakes his head, then speaks as if to himself. "No. I can't imagine . . ." His eyes settle on mine and he asks quietly, "Tell me something. Were you really happy with him or did you sometimes wish . . .?"

I look away from him. "Don't go there."

"I need to know."

I squeeze my eyes, not wanting to recall the bad times. "We were happy at first. But then, something changed. There were times that he wouldn't come home until late or not at all, and . . . I'd be so worried, and then when he finally did come home, he'd smell like liquor. The drinking was a problem, but I just turned a blind eye to it. We had Joey, and . . ."

"I'm sorry. He was a fool to treat you that way. I'm not going to let that happen to you now. Trust me."

I look back up at him, hope and fear warring in my heart, but in my mind, I know I'm the only one who can deal with this problem. And there is only one way. "No one can stop him. I'm going to take Joey and leave. Get my son as far from here as I can."

Wyatt frowns. "That's a violation of your parole."

"What am I supposed to do? Just wait for him to take my boy?"

"The hatchet. It's a problem."

"What do you mean?"

"Maybe it's a warning, but it could be a set-up. What if it's been used in a crime and—"

"He's trying to frame me again," I finish, my gut clenching. I don't know whether to be scared or angry now. "I'll get rid of it. Why give the sheriff something he can use against me?"

"Exactly. But take this stuff to your PO. Tell him everything you've told me. That's where we'll start."

Maybe he's right. "Okay. But if he says I can't leave the area, I'm going anyway."

"You'll get caught."

"I'll change my identity. Disappear. People do it all the time. Lucas did it."

"Look, there's another way. You don't need to leave, uproot Joey, and leave your grandfather behind. Or . . ."

I'm listening, wishing that what he's saying was true.

"If you're right, then he's out there in the woods somewhere. It makes sense. Uncle Sam trained him for it in the Marines. And he lumberjacked these woods for years. He knows every logging road, every hiding place out there. You and your grandfather are probably the only ones who know those woods as well as he does." He takes my hand. "You made the right decision coming here. I'll help you through this, I promise."

"How . . . how can you help me?"

"We'll work together. Find Lucas, bring him to justice, and put all this behind us."

Us? I withdraw my hand, gather the carvings and the knife, and quickly toss them inside the box. "I . . . I don't know. I mean, thank you. I'll think on it."

"You can trust me, Kerry."

I'd trusted Lucas, too, with my heart, my life, and where had that gotten me?

His hand flies to my arm, firmly holding me in place as his gaze locks on mine. He says my name and heat flushes over me, the touch of a man after four drought-filled years makes me ache deep in my core. Something else burns inside me, too, but what? Anger that I'd believed Lucas? Anger that I'd *chosen* Lucas? Anger that I'd run to Wyatt, this man who I'd wronged before, leading him on again when my husband lurks in the shadows of the woods and still in the recesses of my heart?

I start at the thought. Is that true? Does part of me still love a serial killer? No, I hate Lucas for everything he's done to me. To Joey. And to those poor women.

I turn from Wyatt's gaze, but his hand clasps on my chin, turning me back. His lips brush my neck, my jawline, as he whispers my name again and says, "You know that I . . . I've always loved you."

A shudder passes through me, intense desire flows over me, but something dark and frightening heats my cheeks: guilt. Whether it is for wanting Wyatt, the man I've wronged, a man who's not my husband, or for wanting the carnal touch of my murderous husband once again, I don't know. How can I ever know?

I twist away from Wyatt and leave.

Strange Murders: *"The Hatchet Killer"*
Transcript of the original episode, four years ago

Interview with reporter David Wheeler, Valley News: I covered the initial story when the first body part surfaced at the PNT trailhead. I've never covered anything so gruesome. Within hours of the story running, the community gathered in a town hall meeting. A vigilante group formed, and guys took to the woods with weapons. When no one was found, it finally hit people that maybe the killer wasn't a stranger in the woods, but someone from town who had slipped back into their normal lives. Panic set in. It was ugly, the way people looked at each other those days. The shock of it hadn't worn off before the second and then third victims were found. It was like the whole community had been knifed in the stomach. People could barely function, first for the anger, then the fear and suspicion that destroyed our peaceful little town.

FIFTEEN

Adam Nash

I'm naked, in an empty bed, the flesh under my tat burning red and raw. The same as my emotions. I don't know what hurts more, my arm or my heart.

I'd gotten home after nine last night, which was late according to Miranda's ETS. That alone had been enough to put her in a tizzy. But when I'd undressed for my usual and expected task, she noticed the bandage on my arm. I admitted that I'd gotten a tattoo, and her eyes widened with pleasure at first. "A tattoo," she'd purred. "For me?"

That stopped me cold. I had no idea she would ever be turned on by a tattoo. Who knew? There are so many things about that woman I just don't get. But when I peeled back the bandage and showed her the inked eagle, wings spread over my bicep, and talons clenching a banner proudly displaying the word "Mama," she'd exploded with rage, the eleven between her brows pulsating like hot strobes.

"How could you!" she'd screamed. "That woman did nothing for you. She abused you, and yet you put *her* name on your arm? You must be plain stupid, that's what I'm thinking. Plain stupid."

I walked away from her and retreated to my attic, but she'd followed me, invading my personal space. The cruel twist of her mouth is burned into my memory as she snatched up a framed photo of Mama and spewed hateful words. "This woman was no mother to you. Do you hear me? No mother! She was nothing but a lazy, hateful, fat cow."

She flung it toward the floor as she turned to leave.

Now I squeeze my eyes to shut out the memory of her anger, of mine. Good riddance, I'd thought last night. But now, this morning's empty bed, her scent lingering on the pillow, I wonder if it wasn't all a mistake, blown out of proportion in the heat of the moment. I run my fingers over the bandage that covers my permanently inked flesh and realize that I'm lost as to how to fix what I've done. Do I really want to try? Nothing seems to satisfy my wife anymore.

I slide my cell off the nightstand. Seven-thirty. I'm late already and want to go back to sleep, but there's work, and my place is trashed, crap everywhere, my attic sanctuary has been violated, and Miranda is gone. I dial her number, get her voice-mail, and disconnect. There is so much I want to say, but what use would it be to leave a message?

I sigh and push myself out of bed. The floor is cold on my feet as I move to the window, take off my bandage, and study my tat in the light. No matter what Miranda says, I think it's perfect.

That's right, boy. Perfection.

"I knew you'd be pleased, Mama," I mutter while staring out the window at Marco and Rachel's sturdy two-story, brown and beige residence, a sure contender for the least imaginative house award. My gaze pulls toward the second story window and a glimpse of Rachel as she crosses in and out of view, half-naked.

I jerk back, heat flooding me. Embarrassment or something else. Whatever. It doesn't matter and I shake it off. What does matter are those photos she promised to show me of that fateful night at the casino with Lucas and Kerry. I make a mental note to connect with her later. I shower, dress, and exit the house with my thermos filled to the brim.

At the office, Foley leans against Amber's desk, arms folded across his chest, a grim look on his face. It's only Wednesday, midweek, but I'm already exhausted and hoping to catch a quick nap at my desk before going over delinquent parolee files, but he says, "Hendricks was found early this morning, walking down Highway 93, trying to hitch a ride. Seems his truck stalled on one of the back roads. Bird brought him in. He's on edge. Withdrawing, probably. Looks like he's gonna crawl right out of his own skin."

"I'm not surprised. Anything on the Turner woman?"

"Nothing. Search and rescue went back out at daybreak."

I stifle a yawn and swipe my hand over my bicep and Amber flashes a wicked grin my way.

Foley is oblivious to the whole exchange. "See what you can do about getting Hendricks's hearing scheduled soon. We're not set up to keep him here for long."

"Sure. No problem."

"One more thing. The Yates woman is here."

"She is?" My exhaustion evaporates. "Why didn't you say so?" I start down the hall.

"Bird and McCulley's office," he calls after me. "Didn't want her downstairs around Hendricks."

I shift and open the door. She's there, in Bird's chair with a shoebox on her lap. McCulley's there, too, at his desk hunched over his computer, typing. He glances over his shoulder, his gaze sliding from me to her and back to me again. Something's up. I can tell by the haunted look in her eyes. "Give us a minute?" I say to McCulley.

He sighs, flips off his screen, and leaves. I turn my focus to the shoebox, snippets of Weird News Online echoing in my brain: *The severed finger of the third victim was found inside a shopping bag in the backseat of her vehicle.* My nerve ends feel like they're being ground down with sandpaper. "I'm surprised to see you. Our next appointment isn't until . . ."

"Monday, next week."

"Right. So, what brings you by today?"

She hands me the box. As I set it on McCulley's desk and slowly remove the lid, Mama's voice buzzes my brain. *A break's coming, a break's coming, a break . . .*

There's a knife inside, along with a few other odds and ends. Everything looks handmade. The knife is especially well crafted. I go to grab it and stop myself. "What's this stuff?"

"Gifts from Lucas."

My head snaps up. "What?"

"He's not dead. He's still out there. He's been out in the Kootenai this whole time, watching and visiting Joey. What are you going to do about this?"

I lean forward in my chair. "You mean to tell me that he's been seeing the boy?"

"That's not what I said."

"I don't understand. You said—"

"He leaves these things in Joey's treehouse. Joey says he doesn't see Lucas leave them."

"How does he know it's Lucas then?"

"He's sure."

"But how—?"

"I don't know, okay," she snaps back, then sucks in her breath, slides her hard prison face back in place. "But he says it's Lucas. I believe him."

"Is this it? Has he left anything else?"

"No," she answers, but she's a beat too late. Hiding something.

I hold her gaze, trying to wait it out, draw it from her, but she doesn't flinch. "Does he leave notes with these things?"

She blinks. "Notes? No. I don't think so. But last night, Joey heard a noise and thought it was his father. He went into the woods by himself, looking for Lucas."

"Did he find him?"

"Joey says he didn't see him, but he's—"

"He's sure it was him." I sigh and sink back into my chair. There's no real proof that it was Lucas. It could have been anyone.

"Someone was on our property. The barn door was left open and there were footprints at the edge of the woods. Man-sized footprints." She wrung her hands on her lap, her voice panicked. "What if it is Lucas and he's after Joey? What if he takes him?"

I hear Mama's cackle as a future *Strange Murders* title flashes in my brain: *Hatchet Killer Caught Snatching Son*. My temples pound, but I need to keep Kerry calm. "You've been gone a long time. If he was going to abduct your son, he would have done it already." I replace the lid and slide it to the back of the desk, glad that I didn't handle the contents before a lab analysis. Prints could verify that they're from Lucas.

"He's watching us. I've seen some things like lights in the woods by our house. Shadows moving about the trees."

Lucas can't stay away from her. I've already expected that, and this proves it. *This is your chance, boy. Go get him.*

"You don't believe me." She stands, moves to stare out the window, fist balled at her side.

"What? No. I do. I need to talk to Joey, though. There might be something he remembers. But not at your place. Can you bring him here?"

"Here? Is he in trouble? He's just a kid." She turns, her fist touches her center chest now, fearing for her son.

"No. Not at all. I'm just going to ask him a few questions. If Lucas is watching your place, it'd be best if he didn't see me showing up. I don't want to scare him off."

"You don't?"

"No."

Her expression darkens and I'm confused. What did I say?

We stare at each other for a few awkward beats. Finally, she opens her mouth to say something but the door pops open.

McCulley charges in, snatching his jacket from the coat tree in the corner. He crams one arm through a sleeve as he heads back out the door. His face is flushed.

"What's going on?" I ask.

"Call came in."

"The hiker?"

He glances at Kerry. "Amber will fill you in."

Anxiety envelopes me, my stomach churning at the thought of another hacked-up body. I turn back to Kerry, see her clenched jaw; she's pissed.

"You couldn't care less about our safety. You only want to get Lucas."

"That's not true. I do care about—"

"If you can't protect us, then I'm taking Joey and leaving. I won't stay here and let Lucas get to my son. Or put Pops in danger. No one knows Lucas like me. He's dangerous. I can't . . . I won't let him hurt Joey."

Stop her! She's your bait, boy, Mama's voice shrills at me. "Leave and you'll be in violation of your parole. You'll go back to prison."

"What do you want me to do? Sit here and wait to be killed? Or worse, have my son taken away?"

I hold up my palms and speak slowly, reasonably, even as my pulse quickens. "If he wanted to kill you, he would have already done it. My guess is that he sees all of you together again, as a family."

"Your guess? That's the problem. You don't know for sure. You've had four years to track him down and yet he's still out there. Killing again probably."

Killing . . . where did McCulley rush off to so agitated? Bloody red legs and dead white fingers flash in my mind, and I shake it off, but I'm edgy. Not on my game. Exhausted. That stupid fight with Miranda. Why did she have to pull this crap when I'm on the biggest case of my life?

Kerry pushes past me.

"Wait."

She turns back. "What?"

"Don't do anything rash. Yes, I want to find Lucas, but that's the only way you'll ever be fully safe. You and Joey. Give me time to talk to the sheriff. See what he wants to do to help you, protect you. Is there someone you and Joey can stay with? Maybe a friend in town?"

"Yeah right. People like me don't have those types of friends." She slams the door on her way out.

I gingerly touch the throbbing welted word "Mama" now branded on my arm and hear Mama's voice coming in saccharin sweet: *It's okay boy. Just do what Mama says and everything will be okay.*

Strange Murders: *"The Hatchet Killer"*
Transcript of the original episode, four years ago

*On location at trail marker #433, Pacific Northwest Trail
Interview with dog handler Lance Schulz: After the leg was
found, Sheriff Foley mobilized several agencies to aid in the
search. My K9 partner, Ryker, and I were volunteered to help.
Ryker here is a Pitbull/Terrier mix and is one of the best human
remains detection dogs in the state. Anyway, we started at this
mile marker and worked our way outward in grids. The first
couple of hours we came up empty, but then about a mile down
this trail we started hearing birds, a lot of birds, and we hit
on a grassy clearing, and there were about twenty vultures out
there, picking at something. Ryker alerted right away—finding
a human ear, so pecked over I could hardly tell what it was.
Then he found part of a foot, and then . . . well, I spent the
next half hour trying to keep the vultures away until the rest of
the team could get there. I'd never seen anything like it before.
I kept hoping to God that I'd never see that again. Then came
the coroner's results that we didn't find the remains of just one
victim out there, but a mixture of three different bodies.*

SIXTEEN

Adam Nash

"Search and rescue found what looks to be a homicide scene," Amber tells me.

"Damn."

"Yeah. No kidding. Foley's out there already. He dispatched for a crime scene unit. Shouldn't probably say this, but Bird's there, and . . . well, he sounds messed up. It's gotta be bad if Bird's upset. Foleys calling in a cadaver dog team from Libby. You'd better come up with something to say, because Foley's going to want some answers from you."

"Answers?"

"Yeah, dimwit. The Turner girl went missing the same day Kerry was released from prison. And now it looks like we've got another Hatchet Killer victim."

"Sounds like you got it all figured out."

"Get real, Nash. She lived with a man who chopped up women. Maybe helped him. She's evil."

"Maybe I don't see her that way."

"You don't see her that way?" She laughs. It sounds liquidly, like drool leaking from her lips. "She's got you under her spell, doesn't she? You want her."

"What the hell's your problem, Amber?"

Her eyes go wide. "Nothing, it's just that I thought you and me . . . that we had something—"

"Lock this up in evidence, would you?" I hand her a sealed paper back with the box of items Kerry had just given me. I'm not in the mood for Amber's games right now. "I'll take care of it when I get back."

"Did *she* give you this? What is it?"

She stands there, hands gripping the bag at arm's length, eyes glossy, her mouth upturned in anticipation. Her obsession with Kerry is annoying, like a buzzing mosquito that needs to be squashed. "Just lock it up, okay. I'm heading out to the scene."

Thirty minutes later I swipe my forehead and redirect the dashboard vent until a stream of air hits my face. Despite the chill in the air, I'm dripping with sweat. Have been the whole ride out here. The anticipation of the scene, I suppose. Or maybe Amber's accusation: *You want her.* Not true, Amber, you idiot. The only person I want is Lucas. *Get that damn killer, boy.* No matter the cost. I swallow down the acid in my throat and shoot off another text to Miranda—Call me.

Outside, Bird weaves his way through parked vehicles. I cut the engine and step out, catching him as he goes by.

"What are you doing here?" he wants to know. His face is pale and slimy with sweat.

"Got important information for Foley."

"Why not just call him?"

"Tried."

"Can it wait?"

"No."

"Hey, man, I'm telling you, you don't want to go back there. It's bad. Like your worst nightmare."

Images jump into my mind: the green forest floor, Kerry's dead, white naked form, cold, so cold—

"I'll take my chances." I push past him and head into the woods to find Foley, following a trampled trail that leads to a clearing by the river. Foley's there as well as gloved techs hunched down here and there with cameras, baggies and tweezers. He's surprised to see me, but not unwelcoming.

"Search and recovery found what's left of the body about an hour ago," he says, glancing at the dark clouds gripping the sky like long black fingers. "Park Service secured the scene and issued crime scene tech services first. Smart call. Storm's rolling in. We'll need to work fast and get evidence before the rain. I've got a cadaver team on the way."

We're standing outside the perimeter watching the medical examiner pinch up bits of flesh from the rock crevices near the river's edge. There are no discernible body parts, which should make the scene less disturbing to me, but sweat breaks over my body again and my mind goes to the last time I tried to eat pot stickers with chopsticks back in Chicago at one of Miranda's favorite restaurants with red paper lanterns and tiny teapots of green tea on every table. Hated that place. Always felt like a giant at a little girl's tea party. Couldn't get the slippery, crinkled doughy noodles into my mouth with the chopsticks, either. This guy holds up a stringy piece of flesh in front of his face, staring at it, as if he's ready to open wide and—

"The scene's fairly fresh," Foley's saying. "I'm thinking Yates chose this spot near the water so he could clean up after. He had to be covered in blood."

I gag down the puke rising in the back of my throat.

"You don't look so good, Nash."

How many episodes of *The Hatchet Killer* had I watched, imagining this type of scene, but now here I am directly involved and . . . I cough and gag again. "It's all so . . . brutal."

"It's pure evil, that's what it is." He looks at his watch. "I haven't been here all that long. I'm surprised you're here and not still talking to the Yates woman."

"She's why I'm here."

"Oh yeah?" He turns and walks a designated path toward a clump of scrub brush and another cordoned area.

I follow and tell him about the gifts from Lucas. He tips his hat up and surveys the surrounding woods. "So those Hatchet People are right. He's still around here. Has been this whole time, it seems, and her return has triggered another killing."

"Maybe. She's scared for her son. Thinks Lucas is planning to take the kid."

In front of us, a crime scene photographer squats and pulls back the vegetation for a better shot of the bloody blob. "I'm having trouble feeling any sympathy for her," Foley says.

I cup my hand loosely over my mouth and nose, staring at the carrion. "What is that?" I ask.

"Entrails," he says. He turns toward me. "So, the Yates woman told you that Lucas has been leaving things for his boy."

"That's right." I detail the items in the box.

He rocks back on his heels. "As soon as I wrap up here, I'm heading out to pay them a visit. I'll need to you to ride along. We can talk to the boy then." He walks back the way we came, but I stand transfixed. The tech waves a hand over the tall grass, parting it to one side, and I see another part of her mutilated body, discarded with no other purpose than to feed the forest floor.

Strange Murders: *"The Hatchet Killer"*
Transcript of the original episode, four years ago

Interview with Jim Burns, skidder operator, Big Pine Timber:
I'd been skid operating for about fifteen years before Lucas
came onto the job. He was just out of the Marines when he hired
on, and he was a good worker, never late for a shift. Carried
his own weight. I remember we were working a cut-to-length
job up north for the forestry service that day, and I was acting
foreman. It was a rush job, if I remember right, and, well, one
of the guys, his name was Al, was bucking that day, cutting fell
trees into logs. We had an extra cutter out working trying to
get the job done. Anyway, the cutter felled a tree, about a sixty-
foot Douglas, and it was heading right for Al. We were yelling
like crazy, but Al had the chainsaw going and ear protection
. . . (shakes his head) I was on the skidder watching the whole
thing and all I can remember thinking was that Al had a wife
and kids and this couldn't happen. Then Lucas came out of
nowhere and shoved Al out of the way, covering him with his
own body. Both got smacked good by the branches, but the
trunk missed them by inches. No doubt about it, Lucas saved
Al's life that day. And the idea that someone who would do
that, risk his own life for one of his coworkers, and then turn
around and kill a bunch of women, well, it doesn't make sense
to me. It just doesn't add up.

SEVENTEEN

Kerry Grey

"He's a ghost." I'm pacing the floor like a caged animal and Pops is trying to calm me. I move to the front window, part the curtain, and scan the woods. "Sneaking in here and leaving gifts for Joey. Unbelievable. What's going to stop him from coming after Joey? Or killing one of us?"

"Lucas has had a lot of opportunity over the last few years to get Joey. I don't think this is about Joe. I think . . . there's something he wants from you."

"From *me*? He's taken everything already. He's going to get something from me, that's for sure. A bullet in his brain."

A soft scuffle noise from behind makes me cringe. Joey was hiding behind the wall, listening to our conversation and now he's retreating to his room.

What am I thinking, letting him hear his mother talk this way? I survived prison by not trusting anybody, never appearing weak, and wearing a constant mask of invulnerability, but I'd morphed into something darker than when I went in, unrecognizable even to myself. No wonder Joey won't open up to me. Joey loves his father, that's just the nature of things. I know that better than most. I never knew my mother, but I loved her, wanted her desperately in my life, but had to accept that she was never coming back. Growing up, we rarely talked about her, but when we did, I saw the pain wet in Pops eyes. It wasn't my fault that she died, or that's what Pops always said, but hearing it and believing it are two different things, because I knew that if it weren't for me, she never would have been on that operating table in the first place, cut open and bleeding, and then dead. I carried her death my whole childhood, and the pain settled in my gut like a bad seed, took root, grew, branched out and scraped at my insides until over the years all that remained was a hollow shell of a girl, odd, quiet, and peculiar. A girl desperate to feel loved. No wonder I took up with a man like Lucas who poured his desires into me like baptismal water, filling the empty font left by my mother.

I turn to Pops. "At least if Lucas were dead, I'd know Joey was safe."

"Don't talk that way. Joey needs you here, not in prison again."

"And that was Lucas's doing, his fault. How could I have been married to such a monster? How did I not know? What's wrong with me?"

"No one knew. He had a good job lumberjacking and worked hard to take care of you and Joey. He seemed like a good guy. Had us all fooled, that's all."

"Yeah, but you warned way back when I first met him. You told me then, that he was too old for me. Too worldly. So did Wyatt. But . . ." I shake my head at the memory of Lucas's hungry eyes and groping need to have me, fill me, and my shuddering need to feel that ultimate desire of belonging to someone fully. "I was so stupid. If I'd only listened to you, things wouldn't be like this."

Pops touches my shoulder. "That's right. Things wouldn't be like this—we wouldn't have Joey. The boy means everything to you and to me. He needs you. Don't do anything stupid now. Let the sheriff handle Lucas, and you concentrate on your son."

The crunching of gravel draws me back to the window and a white SUV coming up the lane. "It's the cops."

"Why are they here?"

"No idea." Dread chills me. Nash said he'd wait until I brought Joey in for questions.

I step back from the window as Nash gets out of the cruiser first, then Foley. "Stay here," I tell Pops. "I'll take care of this."

I greet them from the porch. "What can I do for you?"

"We need to ask a few questions. And talk to your son," Foley's tone is casual, but his eyes are hard.

I look at Nash. "Thought you wanted us to come into town for that."

"Circumstances have changed." Nash keeps his eyes on my face, waiting for me to respond.

Foley looks over the property, his gaze resting on the woodpile and stump with Pop's axe wedged into the top.

"Like what? What's changed?"

Foley turns back to me, pinning me with a stare. "We found a body in the woods."

"I'm sorry to hear that," Pops says. I turn, surprised to see him standing behind me. "The lost hiker?" he asks.

"Probably. We don't have a definite identity yet."

Pops shakes his head. "Where'd you find her?"

Foley and Nash exchange a look. A sick feeling settles in my gut.

There's a long pause, then I hear Foley say, "We only found part of her."

Pops's face turns pale. I reach out and touch his arm. His skin is icy cold.

Foley's tone changes, his words clipped. "That's why we're here. When did you last hear from your husband, Mrs. Yates?"

"It's Ms. Grey. And not since the day I was arrested."

"No contact since you've been released?"

"Not directly, but I came in and reported some things to Officer Nash this morning."

Nash opens his mouth to say something, but Foley starts in again. "He told me." He looks at Pops. "You didn't know that your grandson was receiving gifts from his father all these years?"

"I did not." Pops straightens his back. "If I'd known, I would have reported it, just like Kerry did. She brought in the stuff as soon as she found it."

Nash nods. Foley asks to talk to Joey.

I bristle. "He doesn't know anything more than what I've already told you."

"It'll just be a few questions. You can stay with him the whole time."

Every muscle in me tightens, but what choice do I have? And I want Lucas found more than anyone. Joey might be the only key to stopping him.

I take a breath and fetch him. He carries his usual bad attitude onto the porch, his eyes, so like his father's, with a glint of defiance, cold and locked down. Foley doesn't stand a chance.

Foley leans down until the two of them are face to face. "Hello there, young man." His smile is anything but genuine. "I'd like to talk to you about your father."

Joey stands tall and says nothing.

"Your mom showed us the things he's been leaving for you over the years. Can you tell me about that?"

He folds his arms and glares at me.

"I had to tell them. I could go back to prison if I didn't." But his eyes take in only my treachery. In his mind, I've betrayed him. I'm a threat to his father, or at least the image he has of his father.

Foley's smile tightens. "Now Joey, it's important that you answer my questions."

Joey's gaze is unflinching.

Foley straightens up, his features dark with anger. "Bet your mother told you not to talk to us. Is that the case, boy?"

I want to set Foley straight, but he wouldn't believe me. There's no use, anyway. Before anyone else can say another word, Joey turns and walks back inside, the cabin door slapping shut behind him.

Foley's jaw twitches. "I've got another dead woman, Grey."

"So you said."

"If you're hiding something, I'll make sure you go back to—"

"I believe her," Nash speaks up. "She's not in touch with Lucas."

"He's right. I'm not hiding anything." I think of the hatchet that was planted in the Bronco. Glad I'd taken Wyatt's advice and pitched it off the Koocanusa Bridge.

"Then you won't mind us looking around."

Pops tenses. "You mean like searching the place? Don't you need a warrant for that?"

"No. Your daughter's a parolee, even so, I wouldn't have trouble getting one. Either way, I'm going to search the place."

"What is this?" I look to Nash. He's fixated on the rotted porch board we've never gotten around to replacing. The creep won't meet my gaze. I'm angry now. I turn back to Foley. "You can't be serious?"

He rocks back on his heels. "You bet I'm serious. Dead serious."

That evening, I move about the cabin packing things I might need for several days on the mountain. Pops follows me. "Don't do this."

"I have no choice." I was stupid and trusted Nash. Tied my own noose taking in those things Lucas left Joey. Maybe even placed a noose around Pop's neck. Foley had asked him a lot of questions, removed and bagged all his hatchets and axes for testing. I'm sure now that Lucas somehow planted that hatchet in our Bronco, but what if Foley found something else? Is that what Lucas wants? To destroy me any way possible? Take away my grandfather, my son, my life? They are my everything. "I plan to do whatever it takes to protect you and Joey. If even it means going back to prison. At least I'll know you two are safe."

"Listen to me, Kerry. The whole time you were down there in Billings, locked away in that place, I . . . every night I prayed for you. I was afraid for you. Your mother's already gone. I can't bear to lose you, too."

"I'll be okay, don't worry. I know these mountains and I'm strong. I'm strong because you've taught me everything I know."

"Then think about your son. I'm old. I'm not going to be around all that much longer. Who will raise him if you're gone?"

Not his father. I'll make sure of it. "It'll be okay, Pops." I wrap my arms around him and inhale his scent, wishing I was a little girl again, here in our cabin, just Pops and me, with my whole life ahead. I'd make so many different decisions. "I'll go say goodbye to Joey."

A knock at the door stops me. Panic seizes me. "Foley," I whisper. "He's back already?"

Pops shakes his head. "Can't be. Would have heard him coming down the lane."

Pops reaches for the door, cracks it open. "Wyatt?"

"I heard that the sheriff was out here earlier. Came over to see how you're all doing."

Pops opens the door wider. The smell of ozone wafts inside. The wind has picked up. I hear thunder. The storm had rumbled north of us all day, and I thought it might pass us over, but now it's gaining steam, coming closer.

"Glad you're here," Pops says. "Talk some sense into Kerry, will you?"

Wyatt's eyes widen when he spies my pack. I sigh, snatch my coat from the peg by the door, and step onto the porch, motioning him to follow.

We settle in the chairs. "What's going on?" he asks.

"It's Lucas. He's killed that hiker and the sheriff suspects I had something to do with it." I quickly tell Wyatt about what happened at the cabin. How the sheriff had searched the place, took most of the hatchets and axes, even a few things from Joey's room. "What if Lucas is setting me up again? Or maybe framing Pops this time. There was that hatchet in our vehicle, but what if I missed something else? All those tools will have Pops's prints on them."

"That's to be expected. They're his tools."

All sorts of scenarios run through my mind. Like Lucas taking one of our hatchets, using gloves while he killed that woman, then planting it back in our barn. I close my eyes. Four years in prison and you hear stuff, know how things can go down. Some women locked up because others planted it that way. Others getting longer sentences because they were uneducated, beaten down by a man or by the system, lacking confidence or the resources to get a good lawyer, and their kids put into the foster system, or worse yet, left to fend for themselves. I couldn't let that happen to me and Joey. Not again.

Lucas maybe wasn't smart, but he was determined and patient. Four years he'd waited; and whatever he had planned over those years was starting now. "I've got to stop Lucas."

"Let me help you."

"No. This is my problem."

"When are you going after him?"

"Tonight."

"In the dark?"

"There's no choice. I know they'll find something to tie the murder to me. Or Pops. And I'll be found an accessory. It's the finger thing all over again, and either I'll be heading back to prison or both Pops and me. And then what will happen to Joey. We'll never have any peace as long as he's still out there."

Wyatt reaches over, as if to take my hand on the rocker arm, but I pull it away. He sighs. "You don't know that. But you do know if you break parole, you will end up back in prison."

"It doesn't matter. All that matters is that Joey's safe from him."

He nods. "Okay. I'll go with—"

"No. But I need to ask you a favor. I need you to look after Joey if something happens to me. Pops is getting older and the stress of all this has been a lot. He needs help."

"This is crazy." He stands, runs his hands through his hair. "You're not doing this alone. There's no way."

"Also I need a rifle, or maybe a handgun. Whatever you have."

"That's a bad idea. It's against your parole conditions."

"That's the least of my problems."

He shakes his head, pacing now. "I can't just give you those. They can be traced back to me."

"Just say they were stolen."

He stops moving, his eyes staring out at the dark forest as the wind blows in air that is damp with promise of rain to come.

"I don't have much time," I say, standing. "Foley will probably be back first thing tomorrow morning. I've got to get away from here."

"The rain?"

"It's not a problem. It's a good thing, actually. It'll wash my tracks."

He turns my way; his voice is steady now. "You remember where we used to meet back in high school? The old tracks, and an abandoned rail car. We'd hauled a pile of blankets back there."

"Yeah. I remember. We were kids."

He reaches out in the dark and brushes the damp hair off my face. "And now we're not."

He leans closer, his face paled by the fractured moonlight spilling onto the porch, and his gaze locks on mine. I want to pull back, whether to not lead him on or to avoid some need inside me or maybe something else entirely, but I want those guns, so I let him kiss me.

And it feels like nothing.

He pulls back and shakes his head. "I'll meet you there with the guns in an hour."

Strange Murders: *"The Hatchet Killer"*
Transcript of the original episode, four years ago

Interview with Wyatt Jones, Kerry Grey's neighbor: Kerry and I grew up together. When we were young, we hung out together mostly outdoors, building forts and fishing, that type of stuff. We were best friends through middle school but lost touch in our teens after she started dating Lucas. As a kid, she was fearless. There was this one time when she risked her life to save a cat that was tangled in fishing line and stranded on the ice-covered lake. Does that sound like a killer to you? I wish I could tell you about that party when she was arrested, but I wasn't around and have no idea what happened that night. But I can guarantee that Kerry is no killer. She's too good-hearted of a person.

EIGHTEEN

Adam Nash

Rachel darts between the puddles forming on the thin strip of grass between her place and mine, meeting me on my front step, a foil-covered dish in her hands. Her hair is loose, wet from the rain and stuck to the sides of her face. "This is for you," she says.

She must have been watching for me to return home. The thought both warms and disturbs me. "What is it?"

"Loaded nacho fries. Thought you might be hungry."

A piece of her hair is stuck on her glossy lips. I playfully brush it off her cheek. "Sounds great. Thank you," I say. Miranda wouldn't approve of the loaded fries, or Rachel, but she's not here, so . . .

"I'm glad I caught you. Heard they found the missing hiker." Her eyes betray her excitement with a sparkling glint. "And that it looks like she was killed by the Hatchet Killer. This proves it, you know. Lucas is still out there. I hate that it's true, but we were right."

We? "I didn't think your husband was all that interested in the Hatchet Killer case."

"I meant you and me."

I warm. Again.

"What was it like? The scene? Was it gruesome?" Her eyes shine as she shakes her head with false pity.

"Very gruesome."

"So horrible. Did he leave anything behind, you know like—"

"Evidence?"

She leans forward.

"Sorry," I say. "I'd tell you, but I can't really discuss the particulars of the case with anyone."

"I completely understand. Anyway, hope you enjoy the nachos. Marco's out of town for a few days. I'm not used to him being gone and made too much. Just thought I'd share with you. And Miranda."

"Miranda's gone, too."

Her brows shoot up. "She is?"

"Spending time with a friend."

"Oh." She peers at me through damp lashes, holding my gaze for a few beats. "You know, I found those photos you were asking about. The ones from the party at the casino the night Kerry was arrested."

My heartbeat quickens. "You did?"

She nods. "Planned to bring them into your office, but since we're here . . ."

"Really? Maybe . . . I guess, that would be . . . I'd really like to see those photos and pick your mind about that night. And whatever you could tell me about Kerry, since you knew her, would be helpful. Hard telling what we'll come up with if we put our brains together."

She shrugs and then smiles again. Her lips are precisely edged in deep rose, filled in with a pink the color of cotton candy. "I like the idea of putting our brains together."

I shift my weight and point to the dish. "Brain food, right?"

"Mmm . . . hmm. I'll go get the photos. Be right back."

Twenty minutes later, I'm licking cheese from my fingers, watching as she bends over, rearranging photos over my dining room table. "I'm putting these in chronological order," she says. "That way you can get an idea of how the evening progressed."

"Good idea. Another beer?"

"That'd be great."

I wander to the kitchen, noting the dishes in the sink. I miss Miranda. At least the way she always takes care of that stuff. A ping of guilt pricks my conscience, but I push it away and open the fridge, reaching past my daily smoothie, another reminder of my ever-efficient wife. She must've premixed one of her fertility specialties, just in case I needed a spur of the moment boost. The liquid is separated now, congealed slimy green globs now floating on pale yellow liquid. I reach past it and snatch two more bottles of beer. "My new virility beverage," I say.

Rachel meets me halfway between the kitchen and family room. "What was that?"

"What?"

"I heard you say something in the kitchen. Were you calling me?"

"No. Talking to myself, I guess."

"Do you do that often?"

"Is this where you analyze me, Ms. Counselor."

"Please. I get enough of that at work." She wraps her lips around the neck of the beer and sucks down a long drink, her eyes fixed on mine.

I look down at my own beer. "Miranda wouldn't approve. Says alcohol kills sperm. We've been trying to start a family."

"I know. She mentioned it a time or two."

I sigh. Of course, she's mentioned it. "It's all she talks about. She's obsessed."

"We all have obsessions. The key to happiness is meeting people with the same passion." She lets her eyes graze over the tabletop of photos, then she zeros in on my lips. One beat, two beats . . .

I clear my throat.

She startles. "Oh, I got the pictures in order. Want to see?"

We move to the table and an electric-like ripple scudders through my skull as I survey the lines of photos, the images flipping through my mind like a cartoon reel. The characters come to life, noises filter into my brain as if I'm there: the glow of neon, the smell of yeasty ale and greasy food, laughter, clinking of glasses, the *bing, bing,* of video poker machines, Kerry and Lucas and Rachel. I recognize a few others, too: the bartender and people who'd testified on the original episode, and . . . "Who's this?"

I point to a picture of a much younger Kerry at a table with another woman. They're leaning, their foreheads almost touching. Kerry's face is rounder and fuller, her hair longer and lighter, her expression serious but not wary and hardened like now. I'm caught up in this moment with her, the lights, the party, the booze. Carefree, young, pretty. No idea that her life is going to change in just a matter of hours.

"That's Dani. Well, Danielle. They worked together at the café downtown. She was older than us by a few years. I don't think she's around here anymore. But maybe she is. I can try to find out."

"Would you do that for me?"

She exhales. "Sure, I would."

"I'm surprised they didn't interview Dani on the show. They were good friends, you say?"

"Best friends."

Best friends share secrets, boy, you know that. My cheeks heat. I hate it that Mama's voice is here. Now. With Rachel here. I block her out, pick up the photo, squint at the image. "I need to know what these two are talking about." *You'd best find*—I cringe, tip back my beer, and gulp down the amber liquid as fast as I can. *You can't drown me out, boy.*

SUSAN FURLONG

"Like hell I can't."

Rachel blinks. "Excuse me?"

"Nothing. Sorry." I finish the beer, wonder if she'd judge me if I went for another.

"You really do talk to yourself. I know someone who might be able to help with that."

I laugh. The alcohol's hit my bloodstream and a numbing warmth muffles Mama's voice to only a faint whisper now, easy to ignore. "I'm good. No worries."

She shrugs and picks up a photo near the end of the lineup. "Check out Kerry's expression in this pic where she's talking to Lucas. She's upset, that's for sure."

The two of them are standing in the hallway at the back of the casino near the restrooms. Kerry's mouth is open, she's jabbing a finger at Lucas's chest. I'd sure like to be a fly on the wall. "Wait. Who's this?" The back door is at the end of the hall and is partially open. A man's standing there. "It looks like he's watching them."

"Let me see." Rachel looks over my shoulder, her breath a hot seesaw on the back of my neck. "Oh. That's just Wyatt. I told you about him the other night."

"Yeah, that's right. I remember. He was the first boyfriend. The one who would have saved her from Lucas had she been smart enough to choose him instead of the monster she married."

"True. Very true. 'Course, we don't always know what we want at first." She hasn't moved away, still lingers behind me. "I counsel a lot of couples who married for the wrong reasons. Maybe money, or convenience, or an ideal image that they had in their mind. The problem is that all that stuff only takes a relationship so far. Things will fizzle fast if they don't share a common interest. Like us."

I turn and look at her. "Us?"

"The Hatchet Killer case. I'm sure you can tell it's an

obsession of mine. Has been for a while. I can't turn it off for some reason. Once you want something, that desire grows. It's common, you know."

"What is?"

She tilts her head with an amused glimmer in her eyes. She takes a half step back, still in my personal space, but allowing me room to breathe. "This . . . uhm . . . type of obsession. I think it's part of the hyper vigilance that results from trauma. This is just my take on it, but before Lucas and the murders, Joy was . . . I mean, we all lived relatively sheltered lives. A great town, good folks, beautiful scenery . . . the murders struck at the heart of our community. We were plunged into a constant state of fear. People's lives changed. They were afraid to go out, be in the woods, hunt, fish . . . who would be next? Their mother, sister, daughter?"

I'd never thought too much about Joy and how it must have been before the Hatchet Killings.

"Thing is," she continues. "People react differently to trauma. Some avoid any association with what has traumatized them. Others rework the trauma over and over, reliving it in order to try to make sense of it."

"So that's why you follow the case so closely. You're trying to rework it in your mind."

"Ultimately, what I want is to be able to go back and stop the trauma from ever happening. But I can't. It is what it is."

"But you can prevent it from happening again. Or you think you can."

She shrugs. "It's no different than people who have lost a child to a drunk driver and they work to make stricter DUI laws. Same thing, really. A lot of folks around here feel the same way."

Yeah, like those crazy Hatchet Club people. My left eye twitches. *Careful, boy. Careful.* I need another beer and a change of subject, but I finally say, "But not Marco?"

She lets out a nervous laugh. "Marco? No. He's not even from this area. Grew up out east, came here to ski. Back in high school my friends and I spent our weekends at The Gold Bar trying to snag ourselves a rich tourist. I got one."

"You seem happy together."

"Always thought we were. At least happy enough. But with all this heating up again, I realize that he'll never fully understand me. He can't because we don't share the connection to this case, the same passion." She steps closer again. "Not like you and me, right . . . *boy*?"

Boy?

Mama? Or did Rachel say that?

I shudder. Rachel? Mama? Outside the rain pelts the windows, rattling the panes, reflecting my own emotional deluge. Rachel is close, too close, and not just her heat-filled body . . . her long candy-pink nails are trying to claw their way into my special world. I don't like this. Not one bit. The Hatchet Killer passion is only between Mama and me. Something special we share. My beer-blurred gaze darts away from Rachel, my brain straining to hear . . . but I've smothered Mama's voice by trying to keep my lustful thoughts from her. Where are you, Mama?

Silence.

Suddenly I want Rachel gone, I need to retreat to my attic, watch *Strange Murders*, reconnect to Mama.

But Rachel's waiting expectantly, her back slightly arched, her breath escaping through barely opened lips. "Can I get you another beer?"

"Afraid I'll have to pass." I smile tightly. "This has been great. Wonderful. I'm glad you came over."

Her lips slacken. "I'm coming on too strong, huh?"

"Wha—? No. Not at all. It's just that I'm tired and—"

"And you're in love with your wife."

No. Maybe. How could I be at this point. "Something like that." I hand her the empty dish and thank her again. "Mind if I keep these photos for a while?"

Her grip tightens on the dish. "No. Not at all." Then a sly smile. "I'll pick them up tomorrow evening. Same time."

She squirms past me and dashes into the rain. I bite my lip as she crosses the yard and disappears into the house. Guilt lingers, and I feel like a boy caught misbehaving.

I'm about to shut the door when my cell rings. I look at the display. "Yeah, Sheriff. What's up?"

"Preliminaries came through on the tools we removed from the Greys' barn. One of the hatchets was positive for human blood. I'm getting a warrant now. For Kerry."

"Severing a body takes a lot of strength, I don't think—"

"I'm not saying she did it on her own. I think she's hooked up with Lucas again."

What was it Rachel had said? People sometimes relive trauma over and over to make sense of it. It seemed illogical to me that Kerry would hook up with Lucas again and relive that nightmare. "Doubtful. I'm thinking it could be a set up. She reported seeing someone out at her place, and don't forget, she voluntarily brought in the gifts that Lucas had been leaving for their son."

"She could have done all that to divert suspicion from herself. All I know is that I've got a hatchet with human blood on it and she's a suspected killer."

"What about Callan, her grandfather? It's his hatchet."

"I don't think he's involved. We haven't seen anything all these years, not until she came back."

How would Kerry react to being arrested again? That was a trauma she certainly wouldn't want to relive. "I want to be there when you pick her up."

"Thought you might. I'm heading out there as soon as the

warrant comes in. Someone's leaked details of the homicide to the local news. I'd like to get out there and pick her up before it explodes in the media."

"Let me know when. I'll be ready."

~ PART II ~

THE SEARCH

Strange Murders: *"The Hatchet Killer"*
Transcript of the original episode, four years ago

Show host, Wesley Steele: The Kootenai Forest covers over two million acres spanning Montana and Idaho and offers some of the most beautiful scenery in the country. For hikers, families, and outdoor enthusiasts, the Kootenai is a massive Garden of Eden. But every leaf has a flipside, and for all the beauty and majesty, there is a darkness to the Kootenai. Like any remote, rustic location, it provides a convenient area to hide evil deeds and evil people. This is where Lucas Yates disappeared after the slaying of three innocent women, and where it's suspected that he remains hidden today. Finding him is like finding a needle in a very large haystack, nearly impossible.

NINETEEN

Kerry Grey

We cross the Lake Koocanusa Bridge on foot at 3:00 a.m. and then wind our way south along a narrow forest service road until we reach Boulder Creek. It's still raining, and my leg muscles burn from slogging through mud. Wyatt trudges behind me, his breath ragged from exertion. I didn't want him to come with me, but he gave me an ultimatum. Either he came or I didn't get the guns, that was the deal. A bad deal. He's slow and cumbersome, and I'd be better off without him.

It's been a while since he's spoken. "You doing okay?" I ask.

His response is garbled. I turn back. His movements are robotic-like, and his eyes two sunken slits in pale skin. Not good. I probably look as bad myself, but my adrenaline has overshadowed my awareness of it. At least for the moment. "There's a place not far from here where we can take shelter and get warmed up."

It was my choice to hike through the night, under the cover of darkness and putting as much distance between us and the sheriff as possible. A mistake, I know now. The temperature is in the low fifties, maybe less in the shelter of the woods. Even with layers of waterproof gear, I'm soaked through, my pants stuck to my thighs and rubbing my skin raw. Wyatt is in the beginning stages of hypothermia and as soon as we stop moving, our body temps will drop even more.

I see the overhang and point it out. We walk that way and shelter under a rock formation jutting out from the side of the hill, just big enough to provide a six-foot-wide dry spot. I'd slept here before, on a summer's night under the stars with Lucas, but I push the memory to the back of my mind and focus on what needs to be done now. I remove my pack and my heavy coat. Cold air stings my sweat slicked body. "We've got to get a fire going."

He doesn't answer, but sits down, his back pressed against the rocky wall.

I tug at his arm. "Get up. You have to keep moving."

He bats my hand away, his eyes half crazed.

He's worse than I thought. There's not much time, so I keep moving. My own legs are heavy, and my body wants to shut down, but I grab as much wood as I can carry, small branches, twigs, whatever I can find. It's wet, but I've got to try. Without a fire, we'll both freeze to death.

I start building the fire just under the overhang, making sure I'm spacing the logs for plenty of oxygen. The rest of the wood I pile nearby, so the heat of the fire will start to dry it. I have cotton balls dipped in Vaseline, and I add them under the tender, using a lighter to spark a small flame. It catches and grows and soon heat licks my face.

I strip off a layer of clothing and turn to tell Wyatt to do the same, but he's sleeping, his head lolled to one side. Getting my camp gear out, I fill a cookpot with the water I have and place it over the fire. Hot liquid is what we need. My fingers ache, and they're a sick white/blue color. I use my knife to strip a nearby pine of a few boughs, shaking off the rain droplets atop them, and lay them out for a bed mat, an extra layer between our sleeping bags and the cold ground.

"Take your clothes off!" I yell. Wyatt startles and fumbles with the zipper on his coat, his eyes glassy and dazed. He's moving slow. Too slow. His lips look chalky white.

I go to him, removing his coat and shirt, and struggle to peel wet pants over his legs. At first, he fights me, then gives up, sinking back into sleep.

The fire is roaring, smoke billowing. I cough and gag as I work to lay out our clothing and get Wyatt into the sleeping bag. He's wearing boxers, and they're like wet tissue paper stuck to his body. I remove those, too. Immediately he burrows into the bag and closes his eyes.

"No, not yet. Stay awake." I need him awake to intake warm fluid.

Filling a mug with hot water, I hold it to his flaccid lips, dribbling some into his mouth. Most runs out, some trickles down his throat. Another couple of sips and then I climb into the bag with him, positioning my body over his.

"Stay with me," I whisper against his ear. He's suspended between sleep and consciousness, a mix of exhaustion and desire in his half-lidded eyes. I check his pulse and it's there, but slow and suddenly, he starts to thrash, his words coming out in grunt like phrases as he tries to push me away.

"No, Wyatt. It'll pass." I know what this is. Confusion. Delirium. And it worries me, because excessive movement is hard on the hypothermic heart. He could go into an irregular rhythm, or worse, heart failure.

I stay put, pressing into him, hoping to calm him and willing my body heat into his. The cold has exhausted me too, my eyelids are heavy. I want to sleep, but the flames grow languid, and I force myself from the sleeping bag to quickly stoke the fire, adding more twigs and a few logs until the fire hisses and cracks. For the next couple hours, I warm him internally with heated water and externally with my body until he begins to shiver, the body's natural way to generate heat, and a good sign that he'll be okay.

As the sun rises on a bleak and gloomy horizon, I finally fall asleep on top of him, my face buried in the crook of his neck, his pulse beating slowly, but steadily against my cheek.

Strange Murders: *"The Hatchet Killer"*
Transcript of the original episode, four years ago

Interview with Lindsey Marshal, sister of third victim: I was three years younger, but we were close. She was good to me, always taking me places, helping me with my homework. I remember when she left for her trip, she was so excited. It was the first time she'd been away from home. She and two of her friends from school had rented a cabin just outside Joy and were planning to spend a whole week there just messing around. I got a text from Abby the day she disappeared. She told me she'd met a guy and he was super cute. She'd made plans to meet him at some bar for dancing later that night and was asking me my opinion on what she should wear. The last text she sent said: "Miss you sis," with a heart and smiley emoji. That was Abby, all heart and smiles. She was the best big sister a person could have. I'll never forget when that sheriff showed up at our place to tell us what happened. My life changed forever that day.

TWENTY

Adam Nash

Callan Grey opens the cabin door and takes a stance, one hand on the jam, the rest of his body blocking the entrance. "What do you want, sheriff? I've got to get my grandson to school."

I'm behind Foley, one step down, wiping my mud-caked boot on the stair board. We've agreed that Foley would do all the talking, while I keep one eye out for Kerry in case she tries to make a break for it.

Foley cranes his neck, trying to see into cabin. "Kerry around? We'd like to talk to her."

"What for?"

"We have some questions for her."

"She's not here."

Foley shifts. "Where is she?"

"I don't know. She was gone when I woke this morning."

I step onto the porch. "Just like that? She didn't say where she was going?"

Callan's gaze slides my way, then back to the sheriff. "The last thing she mentioned was looking for Lucas. I tried to talk her out of it, thought I had, but she felt like she was being set up for another crime that you folks would be more than happy to pin on her. She's gone now. Don't know for sure, but my guess is she's out there tracking him down."

"She didn't mention anything else?" Foley asks. "Like where she thought he might be?"

"No."

"Give me a break. She must've had some idea of where to start looking. There are millions of acres of woods out there."

Callan shrugs. "If she knew, she didn't tell me."

The sheriff steps back, surveys the yard and outbuildings, and the beat-up Ford Bronco parked on a patch of gravel. "She on foot?"

"That Bronco's all we got, so suppose so."

"Is she armed?"

"Not that I know of."

Joey appears behind Callen, hair low on his forehead, a defiant look in his eyes. Foley stoops toward the kid. "Did your mother say anything to you about where she was going?"

"No. Don't care neither. Hope she never comes back."

"Why's that?"

The boy gives him a hard stare. "I want my things back. She should have never given them to you."

"How 'bout you tell me what you know, and I'll see what I can do to get them back for you."

Callan tensed. "Don't be telling the boy to turn on his mother for a box of junk."

Foley raises up and squares off with Callan.

The boy steps between them. "They ain't junk, Pops. And I want them back."

"Hush up, Joey."

He recoils then looks up at Foley. "She went looking for my dad. I heard her leave before the sun came up." He points to the tree line. "I could see the light from her flashlight through the window. She took off that way."

Foley nods. "Fine. That's helpful. You did right telling me. She say anything else?"

Callan gives the kid a little nudge. "Go on now, finish getting ready for school."

He stays put and brushes the flop of hair off his face. "Yeah, she said she was going to put a bullet in his brain."

Foley recoils then recovers his shock.

Callan starts to shut the door, but the kid pushes forward. "You gonna give me back my things now?"

"You bet. Just give me a few days, okay?"

"Move on, Sheriff." Callan's gaze is like steel. "You've done enough here."

"Sure, no problem. We'll just look over there where the boy pointed, then we'll be on our way."

My boots make suction noises on the wet grass as we cross the yard. The dog growls and snarls, the early morning sun glinting off his canines as he charges us. His chain jerks him back, and he lets out a yelp. "You really going to give the kid back his stuff?" I ask Foley, talking over the squawking hens. The sharp ammonia odor of chicken urine creeps up my nostrils, water soaks through to my socks, I need to take a leak. This is a miserable day so far.

"Eventually, maybe. That stuff is evidence, so it's staying locked up for now."

"He thinks you're giving it back soon."

"That's not my problem. Kid's a mess. Give him another five years and we'll be locking him up."

"Optimistic of you."

"Realistic." He scrutinizes the ground along the tree line. "Don't see any tracks. Nothing."

"She's too smart for that. That's why she left during the rain. Her tracks and most of her scent will be washed out."

"Most. Not all. I'll get dogs out here and see if they pick up on anything." He raises his head and looks at the sky. "Can't tell you how many half-frozen folks we pull out of these woods

this time of year. Feels warm to them during the day, but overnight, and with the rain . . ."

"You're underestimating her."

He pulls out his cell and shakes his head. "Sure as hell
hope not. Be a big favor if she was dead, otherwise, we may be
looking at more innocent victims."

We're back in the cruiser when he finally reaches Amber.
"Amber, get ahold of Bird and McCulley. Tell them to meet me
at the . . . who? . . . what are those freaks doing? Armed? With
what? You're not serious . . . Awe hell, that's the last thing I need
right . . . you are? Does anyone else know about this? . . . Keep
it that way." His expression goes somber. "They are? Okay, I'll
be there in twenty minutes to talk to them. In the meantime, put
in a call to Air Search & Rescue. Tell them to be on alert. I'll
follow up with instructions shortly."

He hangs up and starts the engine. "Words out and the
fanatics are on the street in front of the office. They're orga-
nizing, the press is there, it's a damn mess. Allison's parents are
in my office, too, waiting for me. They want answers, like I've
got any for them."

As soon as we turn onto the highway, he flips the lights and
leans forward over the steering wheel, the crow's feet around
his eyes deepening as he squints through his sunglasses. "'Bout
broke me to tell the other victims' families. This girl's parents,
Mike and Angela, they're good people. They took out ads in
every paper, talked to the press, did the social media thing, the
mother, she plastered Allison's face on every trail marker in the
area. They've both been out every day with our search teams,
and now . . . their lives are over now . . . everything they've
worked for, all their happiness, died with their kid, and I can't
even produce a whole body for the coffin. All I got is bits and
pieces." He scrapes his hand through the pewter gray bristles
cropped close to his head. "Hate this part of the job."

I think of Miranda and how badly she wants a kid. I've played along with it, but who in their right mind wants to bring a kid into this world? They take all your time and energy, and then what? All you get back is a bunch of heartache, like the Turners. Or the kid grows up hating you, like Joey. I glance over at Foley, wonder if he's got kids, and decide it's not a good time for that conversation. We ride in silence until we hit Main Street and then slow to almost a stop. A large group, maybe thirty or more people, have gathered on the street in front of the city building, holding signs and chanting, pressing in waves against the front of the building.

Foley takes a quick turn. "We'll go through the back. I want to talk with the parents first."

We enter through the rear entrance leading to my basement office. Hendricks rolls off his bunk and presses his face against the bars. "Hey. When am I getting my lawyer? Why am I even here, huh?"

Foley ignores him and heads to the upstairs offices. "You gotta appoint me counsel," Hendricks calls after him. "I know my rights and—"

"You don't know crap," I say. "Sit down and shut up."

There's a note from Amber on my desk, her handwriting young and loopy: *Dinner tonight?* She wants more than dinner, and I consider what that would be like and guilt twinges deep in my gut. I toss the note into the trash and shoot a text off to Miranda: *Miss you.*

"You might be surprised what I know," Hendricks says.

I ignore him and pull Kerry's mugshot out of my drawer. Foley's kidding himself. Dogs and a chopper aren't going to do anything. We're not going to find her unless she wants to be found. I'd failed as her parole officer. Underestimated her desperation, the lengths she'd go to protect her son. Any good mother would. Kerry was a good mother.

Aren't I a good mother, boy?

"Yes, you are."

"What'd you say?"

My head snaps up, but I don't answer Hendricks. Mama's talking, and I never interrupt Mama. *She's going to find him before you do, boy. You gonna let that happen? You worthless piece—*

"You're a worthless PO, man. Worthless."

"Stop interrupting!" I slap the mug sheet down and storm at the cell. "You hear me?"

He's trouble, boy. Trouble.

"I heard Amber talking and you—"

"You heard Amber talking?"

"Yeah. Heard her say that the Hatchet Killer killed himself another woman. I may know something that could help you."

Trouble. "Oh yeah, what do you think you know?"

"I wanna talk to a lawyer. Make a deal."

"I don't believe you. You're in a bad way, aren't you? You'd say anything to get out and get a fix." I turn back to my desk. Hendricks. The chanting. Too many distractions. I'm not going to get any work done here.

"Did you find the body by the river, where it bends just south of the falls?"

I stop.

He chuckles. "Got your attention now, don't I."

Tread carefully, boy.

"I want a good lawyer. Not some newbie that don't know the law from his ass."

"You telling me that you saw the killer?"

"No. But I saw his car parked out on a loggin' road."

I smirk. "His car? We're talking about the Hatchet Killer, stupid. Lucas Yates doesn't have a vehicle." I turn away. "You got nothing, Hendricks."

I walk back to my desk, pick up Kerry's mugshot sheet and tape it to my reoffender wall.

Strange Murders: *"The Hatchet Killer"*
Transcript of the original episode, four years ago

Interview with Sheriff Foley (continued): We investigated Lucas's background. He grew up in Havre, an only child. He was in middle school when his parents divorced, and he started getting into trouble. By the time he was in high school, he had a record for petty theft, vandalism, a few other minor things. He dropped out of school and eventually went into the Marines. After completing his service, he came here to work for a lumber company and had a few more run-ins with the law. He was on probation for assault. A bar brawl. Seems he had a temper. When we found those body parts, and then that finger in the vehicle registered to him, naturally, we went after him, but he must have been tipped off. By the time we got to his residence, he'd torched the place and ran. There's only one person who knows where he might be hiding, and she's not talking.

TWENTY-ONE

Kerry Grey

I dream of prison: *Gray walls, gray concrete floor, no venti-lation, my jumpsuit like wet, orange skin, the toilet is two feet from my bunk, my cellmate's on it taking a dump, the cell smells like hot crap and my dream-self is irritated. I want to punch her. And then I'm working kitchen detail and it's stew night. Brown and lumpy. Lucas loves stew, but he's not here, he's free, I'm the one rotting in prison, and I stir and stir, more color is what it needs. Carrots, I think, and I grab for one and start to chop, whack, whack, whack, only it's not a carrot, but a finger—my finger!—and blood spurts from my hand. I turn and there is Lucas, hatchet in hand, and suddenly I'm in the woods, running and running and—*

I wake with a start, still melded with Wyatt inside the sleeping bag, his breath seesawing hot on my cheek, steady and strong. The rain has stopped, and the midmorning sun is burning off the clouds. I start to move, and Wyatt's hands clasp around my waist, and his eyes flutter open. "No. Don't," he says. "Stay like this, for a little while longer." He kisses the corner of my mouth lightly, then pushes harder, parting my lips, filling my mouth with his taste.

I sink into him, my body needy and wanting, but my mind telling me to stop. Do I really want Wyatt or just raw sex to quell my fears and fill my emptiness? And then what? Leave Wyatt in the dust as I did before. He doesn't deserve that pain, not again, never deserved it in the first place. What man could handle that rejection again? I start to pull back, conflict raging inside me.

"Don't go," he begs.

"I can't do this."

He keeps one hand on the small of my back, pulling me tighter against him, while his other hand roams toward my breast, his eyes heavy lidded and dark with passion. A wave of heat washes over me as my mind fights for control. I squirm against his hold. "I said 'no.'"

He slides his hand away.

"This just can't happen, Wyatt. Not now." Probably never. My voice sounds harsh in the open air. I try to calm myself. His reaction is normal, expected. Flattering, even. But I don't want to complicate everything right now.

"I'm married." My words shock me. My husband set me up, abandoned me, let me go to prison, broke every vow he'd ever made . . .

"He left you."

"I know."

"He left Joey."

My stomach clenches. "I know." I wiggle out of the bag, cold air slapping my bare skin, just as chilling as Wyatt's words.

"Okay then, if that's the way you want it."

"It is." It isn't, but I can only handle so much at a time. Besides, I'm mad now. *Why does everyone use my heartache about Joey to manipulate me?* I reach for my clothing. "Let's pack up camp."

My body is sore from being tensed against the cold all night. Wyatt moves slowly as he pulls on his clothing. Awkwardness settles between us.

"I was dreaming earlier and dreamt that we found him," I say. "It was so real. Then it turned into a horrible nightmare. He was chasing us through the woods with a hatchet, trying to chop us up." I laugh, but it rings hollow, and my gaze slips to the pistol lying next to our sleeping bag. Wyatt's gun. He also brought a rifle.

Wyatt zips his jacket and squats down to roll the bedding. He's quiet and it makes me nervous. I pull a couple energy bars from my pack. "Want one?"

He takes it and eats it greedily.

Munching on my bar, I stare into the ravine, picking out a trail through the heavy foliage. In my pocket is a gold nugget that Lucas and I had found together. Our insurance, we always said, in case everything went to hell. I'd assumed he'd spent it, or taken it with him, or maybe left it behind with everything else when he torched our house. I was surprised to find it in Joey's box of treasures, but I knew Lucas had left it for me as a way for me to find him.

"It's not far from here," I said. "Maybe an hour or less." I'd told Wyatt about the nugget and that it had come from a small, unnamed creek. Lucas and I'd found it by accident while hunting, out of season. We'd wounded a deer and the blood trail led us to the gulch, the creek, and this nugget. It makes sense that Lucas could hole up near there and not be found. It was remote, a small unknown tributary that wound through dense wilderness, teaming with game, and plenty of places to hide.

As we get near, we plan to split up. We'd talked about it and Wyatt doesn't think that Lucas will come out if we approach the area together. I'll go in alone, carrying the pistol, with Wyatt backing me up, close by with the long-range rifle. I don't know what to expect from my husband. How has this time in the wilderness changed him?

I kneel down, roll my bedding, and feel something brush up

against my back. I turn my head. Wyatt stares down at me. "You haven't told me exactly what you plan to do when we find him."

I stand and tuck the pistol into my waistband. "Whatever it takes. I'm protecting Joey, it's that simple. No matter the cost."

His grip on the rifle tightens. "You talk as if you're going to kill him, but you're still loyal to him, to your marriage. It doesn't make sense."

"I'm not sure of anything. I don't even know for sure that he's out here."

Wyatt squints. "It's odd that he'd leave the nugget with Joey. It's as if he's trying to lure you out here. What if this is a trap and he hurts you? I'd never forgive myself. This whole thing . . . I don't know. Maybe . . . we don't have to do this."

"Don't back out now, Wyatt. I need you."

His expression hardens. "Stop it. You don't need me. You've never needed anyone. Especially not me."

He's angry. I get it. "I . . . I'm sorry. I didn't mean to—" A snapping sound comes from the woods behind us and we crouch down, and listen.

"He's out there," I whisper. "Watching us. I can feel it." I reach for the pistol and grip it in both hands. Leaves rustle, twigs crack and pop, the pistol bounces in my palms.

"Easy. It could have been anything. A deer, some other animal."

I raise a little, peer through my sites into the ravine below, and see nothing, breathe easier, and start to lower the gun when I catch a flash of movement. I swivel right, my finger on the trigger. A deer emerges from the thicket, and I lower the gun and exhale.

Wyatt chuckles. "Told you." He lowers his own rifle, and our gazes connect. We chuckle, a nervous, tight little laugh and the tension between us dissipates.

We finish packing and pick our way along what I believe is a game trail forged by migrating dear or bear. But I know that we might meet up with Lucas at any time. He could be watching us now from the knuckle-like ridge overhead, his sites trained on us, his finger on the trigger. I swipe sweat from my forehead and shiver, as we continue in silence, deeper into the woods until the canopy filters the sun, allowing slivers of light to shine through like lead glass windows. "I hear the creek," I whisper. "It's up ahead."

We cover another hundred feet or so and crouch in the brush. From our vintage point, we can see the creek and beyond. "If he's here, he'd pick a high point not far from the water source," I say.

"It doesn't look like anyone has ever been here. Looks shallow, let's go ahead and cross. See if we can pick up his trail on the other side."

"Current's too strong here and—"

"Look!" He points across the creek to a thin thread of smoke curling up from the tree canopy. "You were right." His voice rises, excited. "I can't believe he's . . . he's here."

He shoulders his rifle, peers down the scope, and checks the magazine as his expression morphs from excitement to fear. My own heart thuds in my chest as my fingers brush against the pistol tucked in my waistband.

As we watch, the smoke grows heavier, more of a ribbon now than a thread. I shield my face and squint. Distance is deceiving in the wilderness; I can't gauge how far—Wyatt brushes past me and toward the bank of the creek.

"Wait!" I hiss, but the rushing water swallows my words. Wyatt motions for me to follow and then lifts his rifle to his chest and wades ankle deep into the water. Panic washes over me. With glacier run-off and rains, the creek the current has stirred up silt and mud. It looks shallow, but the rocks will be slick and dangerous . . . "Wait, don't—!"

I sprint toward him, my hand grasping air as he slips to the left, keeping grip of the rifle by holding it high with his right hand. He cries out in pain. My hand connects to the back of his jacket and I steady him, then see that his foot has slid between two rocks, and his ankle is twisted.

I take the rifle and help him maneuver back to solid ground. He sinks into the dirt, a deep moan rolling from his lips as he grasps his ankle. "It's broken. It's got to be."

I force his hand away and look at his injury. "I don't think so. It's swelling, sprained probably, not broken. Are you hurt anywhere else?"

He shakes his head and cringes.

I glance over my shoulder. Maybe my shouting was heard, maybe not, but we're exposed here, out in the open. "Come on, let's get you to cover." I pick up the rifle and slide my hand under his arm, helping him stand. He leans against me as we make our way back to the trees.

I prop him against the trunk of a pine. He looks at me, and we both know the situation. "I'm not going to be able to keep up with you," he says.

"I'm okay to finish this."

"No. Listen. It's too dangerous to go alone. We know where he is now. We can come back later, with more people."

"Like who? Those Hatchet Club people or whatever they call themselves?"

"No." He moans and rubs his ankle.

"You can't mean the sheriff? Who then? Who's going to help us?"

"I don't know. Just give me some time."

"No. No more time. This is it." I hand him the rifle. "Keep this with you. I've got the other gun. And don't move from this spot. I'll come back for you." I move away from him before he can reach out to stop me. It's better this way, I tell myself. I look

beyond the creek. Smoke is still rising into the sky.
Time to fix this once and for all.

Strange Murders: *"The Hatchet Killer"*
Transcript of the original episode, four years ago

Camera shot of Joy, Montana, Main Street and surrounding mountain ranges. (Ominous music) Show Host Wesley Steele (voice over): The appeal of a good mystery is seeing how the clues come together, solving the puzzle, and serving justice. Unfortunately, real life isn't that simple. Figures show that over forty percent of murder victims and their families go without receiving resolution to their loved one's murder. True crime groupies dedicate themselves to picking up these cases where the authorities leave off, in an attempt to bring closure to the families of murder victims. One such organization has formed here in Joy, Montana—The Hatchet Club. This small but dedicated group of citizens is determined to find and bring Lucas Yates to justice. In the words of their fearless leader, Brax Ryan, "We intend to dissect this case with the sharp edge of facts and tie up the loose ends when we catch this killer."

TWENTY-TWO

Adam Nash

Kerry, Kerry . . . you knew where he was this whole time, didn't you? I slip my EarPods in, and set my favorite rap song on repeat, the heavy base drowning the incessant noise around me: Hendrick's whining, *I want a lawyer, blah, blah, blah.* The chant of the crowd outside, *Blood. On. Your. Hands. Blood. On. Your . . .* And the loudest of all, Mama's voice— *You're worthless, boy, worthless . . .*

I turn up the volume and study the map on my screen. Buoyed by the lyrics and drumming tempo, I zoom in on the map's area around the Grey's cabin. The musician's words echo in me. I close my eyes and let them sink in. *You only get one shot in life.*

One shot, one more shot to find Lucas. "Don't worry, Mama. I'll fix this."

A hand settles on my shoulder. My eyes startle open, and I wheel and turn. Amber stares down at me. I remove my EarPods. "What?"

She flips her hair over her shoulder. "You okay?"

"Just trying to get some work done."

"You were talking about your mother. Meant to ask you about her when you got your tat. Is she somewhere close by? I'd love to meet her."

A shiver runs across my shoulders at the image of Amber and Mama in the same room. "Do you need something?"

"Yeah. Foley told me to come get you. He needs all hands on deck to deal with those Hatchet Club folks outside. They're causing a problem, and word is there's a producer from *Strange Murders* coming to town this evening."

Every muscle in my body tightens. "So soon?"

"Yeah, guess so. Foley wants those people gone before he gets here."

Hendricks calls from his cell, "Amber, come talk to me. I gotta get out of here. You'll help me, right? We used to be friends. Remember?"

Amber rolls her red-rimmed eyes. "I have so many regrets. He's one of the biggest." She pats her too-tight jeans pocket for her perpetual bottle of eye drops, fails to feel it, and rubs a fist over her eyes, smearing her blue eye shadow.

Hendricks goes on. "Don't I mean nothing to you anymore?"

"Shut up!" Then to me. "How long is he going to be here?"

I turn back to my screen and the map. "He may be leaving soon. Bird was saying that Foley might transfer him to county jail in Libby tomorrow and hold him there until his hearing."

Hendricks yells out again. "Can I at least get some food. I'm starving over here."

I glance up at Amber. "Where does the grub come from?"

"We order it in. I'll take care of it." She leans forward and looks over my shoulder. I feel my pulse quicken at the warmth of her breath on my ear and tell myself I don't need to add her to my list of regrets. "It's a big area out there," she says. "Seems to me she must know where she's headed. Nobody goes out in those woods without knowing where they're going."

"Looks that way."

"Don't worry, choppers are going out. They'll spot her."

"Doubtful. She'll know how to stay out of sight."

Hendricks presses forward and shakes the bars. "What's so interesting over there. Come see me, baby."

She straightens, her fist clenched. "Would you be quiet? We're busy trying to find a killer."

"The Hatchet Killer, right? I can help you with that. Come here and I'll tell you all the best hiding places in those woods. I tell you, I seen plenty out there—"

"No one cares what you have to say, Hendricks," I shout.

"Maybe he does know something," Amber whispers.

"He's just trying to get to you. Don't fall for it."

"Okay . . . well, you'd best get upstairs. Foley's expecting you. I'll get Romeo's food ordered. Shouldn't take too long." She lingers a second. "Speaking of . . . did ya get my note? Thought we could grab some dinner tonight?"

I smile up at her. "Not tonight, okay?"

"Oh. Is Miranda back home?"

"No. Not yet." I'd let slip that Miranda was gone, and Amber hadn't let up on it, or on me, since then. "I don't know when she's coming home. I haven't been able to reach her. She's not returning my messages."

She shrugs. "Can't believe she treats you that way. But hey, you've got to eat, right? Just a quick dinner. The Gold Bar has a special tonight, all you can eat—"

"I can't. Not tonight. I'm focusing on the case." I push my chair back, and Amber steps back quickly.

Her expression turns cold. "The case. Right. I understand. Another time, then."

I shut down my computer and stand. "Sure. Another time."

She pouts, but I can't worry about Amber's hurt feelings now. I head upstairs and find Foley, Bird, and McCulley waiting for me. Foley has a bullhorn in one hand, a sheet of paper in the other.

McCulley hands me a vest.

"Is this necessary?" I ask.

"Wear it," Foley says. Then to all of us, "I'll read a brief statement and then ask them to break up the protest. We've already got complaints from the café and a few other businesses. They've got all Main Street clogged up. No pushback, understood. I want to keep this as calm as possible." His voice sounds anything but calm. After effects from his talk with the parents or the pressure mounting from the group outside? Both probably. I don't envy Foley.

We proceed outside to the sidewalk, and the chanters grow louder. *Blood. On. Your. Hands. Blood. On. Your. Hands . . .*

Foley raises the bullhorn. "Listen up!"

Blood. On. Your— "Listen!"

The chant fades as Foley begins reading from his paper. "I'm here to release an official statement from the County Sheriff's Office. Yesterday morning, park rangers notified us of a possible crime scene discovered in the southwest county section of the Kootenai Forrest. We immediately dispatched to the area, and our investigation confirms human remains. Methodology is comparable to that of the killings perpetrated by Lucas Yates. Rangers, out of precaution and safety for citizens, have shut down public access to the national forest preserve, and all park trails in the area, including the Pacific Northwest Trail."

A chorus of boos ring out. "You're just shuttin' us out from going after a killer! We have the right to protect our own!"

Foley raises his hand. "Leave this to the authorities. We can't protect you people and locate Yates."

"You ain't doing nothing to protect us. We've got another dead girl!"

"Yeah, who's next?"

Foley shakes his head. "Listen, we've procured a large ground unit, comprised of federal and local officers, and deputized reserves, all currently searching for Yates. I assure you that we are doing everything possible to find him and bring him to justice. We are asking that you please disassemble, so that we can more effectively do our jobs."

A voice cries out, "You haven't done your job for years, Sheriff!" And another, "How many more girls have to die?"

I scan the crowd. Brax is up front holding a sign that reads, *Lucas Yates, Wanted Dead or Alive*. Only the word *Alive* is crossed out. He shouts out, "Was it Allison Turner?"

Someone else yells. "Who else is gonna die before you can find this guy? We demand access to those trails."

Then Brax's voice again, "If you can't do it, Sheriff, then get out of the way and let us find him."

The chant starts again. *Blood. On. Your. Hands. Blood. On. Your. Hands.* One voice rises above the others and my gaze is drawn to the middle of the crowd and a petite brunette. Rachel! Our gazes lock. Her lips curl up into a wicked little grin. *My, my, my . . .* so she *is* part of the Hatchet Club. She somehow forgot to mention that fact. Makes sense, though. She's as obsessed with the crime as I am.

She bends down and picks something out of a canvass bag and heaves it at Foley. A scream pierces the air as it hits the ground and bounces at his feet. A bloody hand!

I do a double take. No, not a hand, but a latex glove blown up and tied off and covered in blood, animal blood, or more than likely red paint.

Another flies through the air, and another. Foley pulls back and covers his faces as one hits him square in the chest, red paint smearing over his shirt, splattering his neck and chin. Others hit the brick wall, the sidewalk, the windows, and it's starting to look like a massacre. Foley ducks into the building; Bird and McCulley move into the ruckus and start cuffing people; I leave my post and head into the street. The crowd is no longer a tightly formed cluster, but a chaotic web of bodies, disbursed in all directions. Some seem intent on still chanting, but the words are lost as others scurry off like roaches caught in the light. I catch a glimpse of Rachel running into the alley across the street and go after her.

"Hold up, Rachel!"

She stops and turns, doubling forward as she catches her breath. "Are you going to arrest me?"

"You didn't tell me you were part of the Hatchet Club."

"You didn't ask. Why?" She stands upright and looks me square in the eye, her gaze both guilty and hopeful. "Do you think less of me now that you know?"

"Your group makes it hard for the real cops to do their jobs."

"That wouldn't be the case if they would simply work with us."

"Work with you? The way you operate? You people sent a bloody leg to our office."

"Only because they shut us down at every turn. Brax says—"

I snap back, "Don't listen to what that guy says. He's an idiot."

"And Foley's not?"

We both pause the moment, eying each other. Two combatants but on the same team. Both of us want the same prize: Lucas.

"He's doing everything he can. It's not that easy."

A breeze blows down the alley, kicking up trash spilled over from a nearby dumpster. She pulls her sweatshirt tighter. "You moved here to find him, didn't you? Don't bother denying it. I see the obsession in your eyes every time I mention his name. What I don't know is why. Is it personal? Did you know one of the victims? Your sister maybe? Girlfriend?"

Careful, boy, she's a clever one. "I moved here because I was hired for a job."

"I don't believe that for a second. Partner with me. I can help you. I've lived here my whole life. I know the people—"

"I already have a partner."

She snorts. "Miranda? She's not much of a partner these days, is she?"

I meant Mama, but she wouldn't understand, so I let it go.

"And she doesn't share your passion for finding Lucas. It's obvious." She cocks her head. "And I can imagine that it's driving a wedge between the two of you."

"Good guess, counselor. But that's our business, not yours. What I don't get is what's really in this for you? And don't give me some cock and bull story about passion and righting old wrongs. I'm not buying it."

She looks down at her feet. "Okay, truth is, things between Marco and I aren't as great as they seem. He's got a problem. A gambling problem. And we're in over our heads."

"Did he put you up to this? Did he tell you to kiss up to me so that you could get official information to help you find Lucas before the others?"

Her head snaps up, her eyes glinting with disappointment tinged with anger. "No. He has no idea that we're working together on this."

"We're not working together."

"Really? I brought you the photos. And I found out about Dani White Elk."

My interest piques. "White Elk? That's the friend's last name?"

"Yeah. She quit the café a few years ago. Works for one of the lumber companies now. No one's sure which one, but she's still in the area. People have seen her around town." She steps a little closer, anticipating that we might work together. "Do you want me to see if I can track her down? She'd be more willing to talk to me since I'm from this area, or . . . we could interview her together."

She's waiting, a glimpse of hunger in her eyes as she subconsciously licks her lips. She's lied twice about her need to solve this case; it isn't some altruistic way to "save the lives of future victims" nor would this independent career woman put herself out to pay off the debts of her jock husband she now regrets as a mistake. No, there is something more. Something deep and visceral. Maybe solving this case is a way to prove her self-worth to others. Or to herself. That same ache stirs in me, and I wonder what it would be like for us to work together, sharing this passion, fulfilling that hunger. Partners . . .

Don't be stupid, boy. She'll use you, just like that no-good wife of yours.

"That might be useful," I say. "Can you talk to her and let me know what you find out? I've got bigger things that I need to take care of right now."

"Yeah? Like what?" Her eyes widen. She leans forward.

You're such a fool, boy. "I can't talk now, I've got to get back to work, but see what you can find out from White Elk and come by tonight. We'll figure out something then."

Rachel's sly smile is back. "I like the way that sounds."

Strange Murders: *"The Hatchet Killer"*
Transcript of the original episode, four years ago

Interview: Jay Stacker, neighbor. I lived out by where Lucas Yates and his wife lived. We were the closest neighbors in that area. I'll never forget that night. It was after midnight when a loud explosion woke me. I threw on clothes and ran outside to see what had happened. I could see the flames through the trees. Lucas's place was on fire. I ran to see if he needed help and there he was, standing there with a gas can in his hand watching his place burn. I called out to him, and he turned and looked at me, and I swear to God, he looked like a crazed man. It still gives me shivers when I think about the look in his eyes that night. And you know, he didn't say a damn word, just tossed the gas can and disappeared into the woods. That was the last I'd seen of him.

TWENTY-THREE

Kerry Grey

Perhaps I should listen to Wyatt, turn back and play it safe, but I want to finish this nightmare one way or the other and bury my past forever.

I backtrack, keeping low, and eye the smoke lazily rising from somewhere beyond the other side of the roaring creek. Removing my boots and socks, I scan the swirling water for a safe place to cross. On the other side, I slip my footwear back on and start upstream searching for signs of Lucas.

Finally, I spot a couple overturned stones, their surfaces covered with fresh dirt, then a patch of grass, the blades bent and pointing straight ahead to a penetration point into the underbrush of the woods.

The path is steep, and my legs strain as I ascend. At the top, I pause and look down. Rocky ledges below me hang over the area, but as I lean a bit, I see they cover a gulch in a valley. Obscured, but in plain sight if you just look close enough. Lucas's lair?

I glance at the ground and see signs of human activity everywhere now: freshly broken twigs, trampled dirt and grass. Lucas knows these woods better than anyone. He'd successively evaded capture for four years, remaining invisible to air and ground searches, knowing to avoid leaving such obvious signs.

These visible signs were probably left for my benefit—a trap. But I can't stop, won't stop, so I continue following the path that now angles down the mountainside to a small lean-to protruding from the rocky wall of the mountain—half-cave, half-shack—suddenly comes into view. I stop, step back out of sight and a hand clasps over my mouth. It tastes dirty and bitter and pulls me back until I'm pressed against another body, this one muscular and familiar. His grip is tight, one hand on my face, the other around my chest. "Shhh. Kerry, shhh. It's me, Lucas."

Panic surges through me at the sound of his voice. I squirm and kick, and spin away. I catch a glimpse of his long beard, wild eyes, and scream out for Wyatt, my fingers reaching down, grasping and fumbling over the pistol tucked in my waistband. Finally, I connect to the grip. I draw and aim upward, but his one hand grasps my arm and pushes the gun away, while the other hand, now a fist, swings at my face. The blow knocks me backward, the gun falls to the ground, and I'm consumed by darkness.

I wake to the sound of rain against the crude walls of the structure, the smell of woodsmoke, and soft fur underneath me. My face hurts, my neck is stiff, and I'm bootless. I blink, turn my head slightly and focus on Lucas. He's seated not far from the fireplace, but between me and the door. His shirt is off, the pistol in his waistband, a basin of steaming water next to him. He dips his hands and splashes water over his face and shoulders. I remain still and survey the simple room: a primitive wood table, some shelves stocked with provisions, furs, rough tools, and I slide my gaze back to the pistol. Could I—

He's staring straight at me. "I know you're awake, Kerry."

"Lucas." My voice is dry and horse, my throat like dust.

He dries his face and points to a stainless-steel bucket on the table. "There's fresh drinking water in there."

I hoist myself up, cross the room and cup my hand, dipping and drinking greedily.

"Why have you come up here?"

I stop and look up. Lucas stands over me, his shirtless torso well defined. Up close, I see how much his face has been darkened and weathered by the sun. Lines radiate from his intense blue eyes now, and his once closely cropped hair is wild and long. He's too close, and fear kicks up in me. The door is behind him and there's nothing for me to use as a weapon. I can't run for it; my boots are gone. Where are my boots? And he's quicker and stronger and would easily overcome me. "You drew me up here. Don't pretend you didn't. The gifts to Joey . . . the nugget we found together in the creek." It's buried deep in my pocket, and I keep it there. I can't afford for Lucas to take it back.

He smiles slightly. As if it's all coming together in his favor. Maybe it is.

I continue to search the peripheral for a weapon and spy my boots in the corner by the fireplace.

"Is Joey okay?"

My gaze snaps back. "You know he is. You've been watching us."

He doesn't deny it. "Are you here to collect on the bounty money, or did you come for another reason?"

Anger swells inside me, its taste bitter and overpowering. "I went to prison because of you."

"I know you didn't come up here alone. Where's Wyatt?"

"I missed four years of our son's life."

"I'm sorry about that. Where's Wyatt? He's not what you think—"

"Did you hear me? Our son is ten now. I missed all that time with him."

He steps forward, reaches out. "Listen to me. I'm sorry, but—"

Like hell he is. I can and will kill him.

I make a dive for the gun. But he snatches my arm and pushes forward. We both tumble to the floor, him on top. I squirm and kick, but he shifts his body to immobilize my legs and pins my hands above my head.

His face is calm, his gaze clear, his body heavy on mine. "I did lure you up here. I took a risk that you might believe me."

"Why would I believe anything you say. You've lied to me all along."

"No, it wasn't me. You have to tell Joey that it wasn't me."

"Everyone says it was you. Now get off me."

"Listen to me. That night the cops pulled you over and found that stuff in the car you were driving. Why would I do that? The car was mine. Why would I be so stupid as to leave evidence like that in my own car? Think about it."

"Think about it? It's all I've thought about for the past four years. How you let me take the fall for something I knew nothing about."

"I didn't know that. When I first heard the news, those women . . . I . . . I knew them . . . and I thought you . . ."

A chill hits me and I stop struggling. "You thought I really was Killer Kerry."

He stares at me, says nothing, but moves off me. We stay seated on the floor, glaring at each other.

He thought I was the Hatchet Killer? A little voice in my mind whispers, *turnabout is fair play.* I ignore it. "They tied you to each girl," I say. Even now it still hurts to say it. "You didn't just *know* them, you slept with them."

"I'm sorry. I'm sorry that I hurt you that way. We were young . . . and I—"

"Stop with the excuses." My voice is shrill, my mind vacillating.

"Kerry, we had something special, something passionate

beyond any affection you could have with Wyatt, and you knew that. But still you never got over him, the rich boy, the good boy. I knew it all along. I felt like I didn't measure up to him. The other women, they were a way to even the score."

"Don't blame your infidelity on me." I bite out each word, my mind slow, crazed with unwanted memories. How many nights had I waited up for Lucas, only to have him come home half-drunk and smelling like another woman? The whole town knew about his affairs and one night stands. Wyatt knew. That night when he showed up at the party, he told me that Lucas had been cheating on me, like I didn't already suspect it. Wyatt was sympathetic, supportive, a good friend.

"You torched our home and disappeared."

"What choice did I have?"

"There's always a choice. You picked the one easiest for you."

"Did I? I know I didn't do it, but the cops weren't going to even consider other suspects besides me. They never would have, and you know that."

"Why should they?"

"Because I'm innocent." He grabs my arms. "For a long time, I thought you were guilty. That you'd gone after those women and planned to frame me for it, and somehow your plan went wrong. But then I got thinking about Wyatt and the fact that he was always hanging around you. He never got over you, and when you married me, it was like something in him snapped. Think about that night, Kerry. About my car."

A 1984 Camaro, completely restored, perfect condition, with a top end stereo system. He never let anyone drive it, rarely me, and always kept it locked. I didn't even have a key for it. "Yeah. It was your baby." I hated that car.

"You took it that night to piss me off."

"So? I was your wife and it was late. I needed to pick Joey

up from Pops's place and get home. You were too drunk to drive anyway."

"And you knew I had a key hidden on the undercarriage. Did you tell Wyatt? Or was he there with you when you took the car?"

My mind whirls as I recall reaching under the grungy fender, groping for the key. It wasn't in the usual spot. I had to search underneath the whole fender. Had Wyatt used the key and . . . "What? What are you saying?" It can't be true. No matter what Lucas thinks, Wyatt didn't kill those women. He didn't plant that finger. He's not capable of those types of things.

But Lucas is right about one thing . . . I gave up so much, I gave up Wyatt for Lucas, traded stability and wealth and love for passion and excitement, and with it, heartache and a dirt-poor life. But even at that, I'd been loyal. And how did Lucas repay me? By betraying me with those women. I'll never forgive him for that. Never! Men like Lucas never change. But Wyatt is nothing like him. Wyatt isn't a cheater or a murderer . . . I know better. "You're lying to me just like you always have."

"What other options are there, Kerry? Someone planted that finger, and Wyatt was always hanging around you, watching for his opportunities. Bet he was there the night you took off in my Camaro, wasn't he? He could've tossed the bag in the backseat after he smooth-talked you, and you never would've known. We were all so drunk that night, Kerry. Implicating me in a crime like that would've put me out of your life forever, made room for him."

"No! Wyatt didn't kill those women." My mind sickens at the thought of blood on Wyatt's hands.

"Why not? Your jilted lover boy might do anything to . . . or . . .?" His eyes grow wide as if he sees something fearful through the window. His expression hardens, his muscles tense, as he shoves me aside and lunges for the gun just as the door smashes open.

Wyatt bursts in with the rifle in his hand, a shot fires, the sound shatters my eardrums, something wet splatters over me, Lucas's blood, and he crumples to the floor, blood and saliva gurgling from his throat, his skin draining of color.

I kneel over him, wanting, wanting . . . what? I've wanted him dead these last four years, and now I watch in horror as life drains from him. I know now that I never wanted him dead. His gaze rolls my way, already taking on that milky look. I lean in closer as he struggles to make words, and he says, "Tell Joey the truth." He goes limp.

I hear a sharp intake of breath behind me, and I look up, straight into the barrel of Wyatt's rifle. "He's dead," I say. "You . . . you killed him."

The barrel bounces just inches from my face. Wyatt's voice shakes as he speaks. "He was going to kill you."

I work hard to maintain eye contact, but every fiber of me is focused on that rifle. Wyatt holds the weapon that just killed my husband, it's barrel still aimed at me. Why? I thought I knew Wyatt, could count on him, but now . . . I skim the ground, searching for the gun as I slowly rise. I can't find it. Wouldn't do any good if I could. Wyatt has the rifle trained on me, the barrel following my movements as I inch closer.

He's somber, his gaze flickering as if trying to reconcile the facts.

I keep talking. "How did you get across the river? Your injuries?"

"I had to . . . to protect you."

I nod. "And you did." The police would come, easily accept that Lucas had threatened me, and Wyatt had followed to protect me. Just like always. Watching and protecting. No one would believe Lucas's profession of innocence or his indictment of Wyatt, a pillar of the community, lovelorn and protective. It would be over. But . . . an ice-cold shiver runs up my back. Lucas's words ring in my mind; Wyatt was at the bar that night, seeing me to the car, just as Lucas suspected. "Wyatt. Put the gun down."

"I don't know if I should." He takes a half step back. "I was at the door and heard you two talking about that night. About the key to his car. About other options." His soft brown eyes moisten with sadness.

We both know the truth. A thousand thoughts scramble through my mind as the rifle bounces in his hand. "Please put the gun down."

He tightens his grip and stares at Lucas's dead form, his eyes puzzling over what he's heard and the consequences to come.

My PO's words come back to me, "You've crossed a Rubicon." That's what this is. Wyatt and I have crossed a Rubicon, there's no way back, only forward. I have to survive. For Joey.

I throw myself at him. He stumbles, his back hits the wall, and the rifle falls to the floor. We both scramble for it, my hands connecting to the stock, his to the barrel. He yanks and jerks me off balance. I fall into him, we both fall, and there's a sickening *thunk* as Wyatt's head strikes the edge of the fireplace hearth. I roll away and stand over him, holding the gun and looking down at his still body, blood already oozing from his skull, his eyes wide open and unmoving. The scene overwhelms me. My body trembles as I cram my feet into my boots and grab my coat. I stumble out the cabin door, sucking in gulps of air, and then retching and dry heaving until I'm inside out. *Both of them dead? Both of them . . .* horror and panic surge through me. And I run.

Strange Murders: *"The Hatchet Killer"*
Transcript of the original episode, four years ago

Interview with Lana Reece, friend of victim Abby Marshal: That day I had a creepy feeling. I couldn't quite place it, just something seemed off. We spent the morning walking around town, then we bought some supplies and packed a picnic lunch. The whole time, I had this feeling that we were being followed. I mentioned it to Abby, told her that it felt like we were being stalked, but she just laughed it off. Later, we headed out to Lake Koocanusa. Abby was the crazy one in the group, but in a good way, you know? Well, that day she insisted on skinny dipping in the lake. I didn't want to, not at first anyway, but there wasn't anyone else around and it seemed okay. She said it was like one of those things you'd always remember and laugh about later. But as soon as we stripped down and got in the water, I saw a man in the woods, watching us. I couldn't make out his face for all the shadows, but it was scary, the way he just stood there, watching. I pointed him out to Abby, and she just giggled and, I couldn't believe it, but she waved at the guy. He instantly backed away and disappeared into the foliage. To this day I wonder if he targeted her because of that wave. I mean, he could have decided to come after me instead, right? Because when I look back on it, I figure that was the Hatchet Killer choosing his next victim.

TWENTY-FOUR

Adam Nash

My tires rumble over the cattle guard and dust kicks up behind my vehicle as I drive down Wyatt's lane. It's after six already. As soon as I'm done here, I'm getting take-out from The Gold Bar. We'd ordered their prospector's special—cheeseburger with chili, fries, and coleslaw—delivered for Hendricks before I left the office, and it looked good. Surely not a Miranda-approved meal, but my recent changes agreed with me. I've never felt better.

Wyatt's ranch is on a long stretch of land about three miles from where the Greys live. The house is a large two-story log home, with a green metal roof and long porch with rockers and potted ferns. It's neat as a pin, stately, and eerily quiet. I knock and listen, and walk the length of the porch, my loafers silent on the wood planks. A warm breeze carries an earthy smell laced with sweet mountain laurel, the tinkling of wind chimes and distant echoes of lowing cattle. It's peaceful, but isolated. How can a man can stand to live so alone? And then I think of Miranda and our fight, and now our separation, and feel a stab of regret, but it goes as quickly as it came, and is easily replaced with anticipation of Rachel's visit later tonight.

I descend the porch steps and walk around the side of the house. The windows are dark and empty. No sign of Wyatt

anywhere. Curiosity pulls me toward the barn, an older structure, with a stone foundation, hayloft door, and a cupola
topping the roof. The type of barn you never see anymore. I
cup my hands against a dusty window and hear a scratching
sound and a long moan, and I imagine Kerry tied and bound, or
injured, maybe even half-dead.

I scurry around to the double door. It's swollen, but I
manage to slide it open a smidge and squeeze through sideways.
A swallow swoops overhead, then another. A mixture of moldy
hay and the sharp ammonia-like smell of urine wafts over me. I
cough and gag and move past the adjacent wall where horse tack
and grooming tools hang from hooks, and work my way to the
back of the barn, to the horse stalls, and the source of the noise
I'd heard earlier: not Kerry, or any human, but a pig, snorting
down grain from a time release feeder. It pauses and lifts its snout
my way, sniffing the air before it goes back to eating.

Next to the stall is a door with a latch and padlock. Chemi-
cals, dangerous implements, there are probably a ton of things that
need to be locked up on a ranch, but . . . my interest is instantly
piqued, and I find that the padlock isn't fully latched. I wriggle it
free and swing the door open, my eyes adjusting to the low light
and the scene before me. My breath catches in my throat.

Photos of Kerry. Everywhere. Not just a few, but hundreds.
Kerry both as a young woman and now. And not poses, or
selfies, or whatever people call them these days. These are
stalker photos. Shots of her in unsuspecting circumstances:
shopping, hanging clothes on the line, talking with other people
whose images have been cut off. Long shots, close-ups, some
blown up to blurry sizes.

I dial Foley. "I'm at Wyatt Jones's place."

"Why?"

"Someone told me that he and Kerry were close. I thought
he'd know something about where she might have gone."

"Did he?"

"He's not here. But there's something you should look at in his barn." I describe what I'm looking at. "It's a shrine like you'd see in a stalker movie."

There's a long pause on the other end. "Why'd you go in the barn?"

"Thought I heard someone inside. Someone in danger. Thought maybe it was Kerry." I wait for his response, but he's silent. "Foley, you there?"

"Yeah. I'm thinking."

"Do you want to send someone out here to look at this?"

Again, silence, except for the sound of a siren in the background.

"What's going on?"

"I'm at the county hospital. They're bringing in a woman. A hiker, in bad shape, but alive. Her description fits Allison Turner."

"The hiker, but how—?"

"Hell if I know."

I think about what Hendrick's said earlier about seeing a vehicle parked on the logging road not far from where we found the crime scene. Who knows what this habitual small-time criminal really saw out there in the woods? The guy shoots his mouth off about stuff all the time, most of it not true, no one believes anything he says. "McCulley and Bird?"

"They're both tied up right now."

"What do you want me to do about this?"

"Put things back the way you found them and leave. I'll go out there and have a talk with him as soon as I can get away from here." The siren grows louder. "I've got to go. I'll be in touch."

Strange Murders: *"The Hatchet Killer"*
Transcript of the original episode, four years ago

Interview with Sheila Berg, MD, FAPA (continued): Basically, serial murderers can be categorized into four major types according to their motivation for killing: the visionary killer, who believes he's seeing visions or hearing voices telling him to kill; the mission-oriented killer, who is determined to eliminate a certain type of people, such as prostitutes; the hedonistic killer, who simply derives pleasure from killing; and the power-hungry killer who is motivated by exerting control over a helpless victim. It is, however, possible for the killer to fall into two or more of these categories, which I believe is the case of the Hatchet Killer. I base that on various factors, including the brutality of the murders, the extent of dismemberment and location where the remains were found. Serial killers often sexually assault their victims as both a physical and psychological component of the murder, and sexual assault may be present in all four categories of motive.

Interview with Chet Hanson, Lewis County Deputy Coroner (continued): We were unable to determine if the victims were sexually assaulted. The bodies underwent prolonged postmortem intervals, with destruction or deterioration of evidence due to environmental conditions like heat and rain, insect infestation, and animal damage, all contributing to an increased rate of decomposition and an overall loss of viable subject testing matter. In other words, crime scene investigators were unable to recover intact torsos, or the necessary female anatomy required to make such a determination. Overall, the DNA evidence that we were able to collect from the scene did not result in a usable DNA profile, so we knew from the start that DNA wouldn't play a big part in bringing this monster to justice.

TWENTY-FIVE

Adam Nash

Rachel lounges next to me on the sofa. She showed up around midnight dressed in yoga pants and an oversized sweatshirt that continually slips off her shoulder. We've been talking for hours about true crime documentaries, favorite podcasts, and our "passions." Recently the conversation has turned to the real reason she's here: to find out about the Yates case. But I'm tired of talking. I'm ready for something else.

I maneuver closer, pushing her against the cushion, but she squirms out from under me. "Slow down," her voice is husky, demanding. "I want to know more."

"I've told you everything."

"The photos at Wyatt's place. How many do you think there were?"

"Hundreds."

"A man obsessed. I knew it. There's always been something off about him."

I look beyond her and out the living room window and survey the neighborhood. It's early Friday, maybe two or three in the morning, houses are dark. I should send Rachel home, but I'm still hopeful for something more. Pressure and frustration mount inside me. Kerry's disappearance, my own inadequacy in resolving the case, Miranda leaving me, and now Rachel's teasing.

I make another move and she wiggles out of my grip. "Do you think it's possible that everyone has been wrong about Lucas?" Suddenly her excitement wanes and she says, "So all this time, looking for Lucas, and even if I found him, I wouldn't get—but, wait. The reward money still goes to anyone who provides information leading to the capture of the Hatchet Killer, even if it isn't Lucas, right?"

"I don't know the particulars."

"Those photos I gave you, they're evidence that Wyatt was at the party that night. That could be crucial to building a case against him if it turns out to be him."

"We don't know who the Hatchet Killer is yet."

She ignores me and is on a roll again. "And Wyatt was there that night. We know that for sure. He could have put the finger in the car. Lucas's car. To frame him. He didn't know that Kerry would be driving it that night."

I'd already thought of that. How ironic that would be. In an attempt to take Kerry for his own, he got her carted off to jail for four years.

"And the first killings. That summer . . . oh, I never thought of this."

She pushes up and gets to her feet, starts pacing, leaves me behind on the sofa alone. Irritation takes over. She's slipped into her professional mode. Counselor mode. I've seen it a few times this past week. A seriousness settling in her expression, that focused look, and . . . and an eleven between her eyes.

You've gone and done it again, boy. Got yourself another loser.

I grit my teeth. "What? What haven't you thought of?"

"The pieces are falling together now. Don't you see? It must have been torture for Wyatt to watch Kerry and Lucas build a life together. He must've finally snapped. The woman he loved married another man and . . . oh, my gosh. Those woman . . . they . . . did they all look like Kerry?"

My face burns hot. Like I haven't thought of these things. Who does she think she's talking to? "No. Emily Lynn was a blonde."

"Huh? A natural blonde, do you think?" Her gestures become flamboyant. "Organized killings, that's what we're looking at. Like Ted Bundy. Fueled by early childhood trauma and set into motion by rejection. It was never Lucas. We were wrong. We were all wrong."

You going to let her talk to you like that, boy. She doesn't know crap. She's nothing but a cheating little tramp and you're . . .

Rachel stops and wheels my way. "And Allison Turner fits the same profile as the others."

A laugh bursts out of me, an instant release to my frustrations.

Rachel glares at me. "Why are you laughing? What's so funny?"

"You. You don't have all the facts. It's not your fault, you're just not . . ."

Mama's little detective.

"What? I'm not what? You think I'm stupid?"

"No! You just aren't privy to the same information as I am. But you know that, don't you? That's why you're hanging around me so much." I pat the sofa cushion next to me.

She folds her arms and shakes her head.

I pick a piece of lint off the fabric. It isn't like she won't hear in the morning anyway, so I appease her anger by relaying the update I got from Foley. "Allison Turner isn't dead. She's very much alive and recovering at County Hospital. Unfortunately, she's lost a finger or two, and her big toe. Exposure, not from a hatchet blade."

"Then who . . .?"

"I don't know. Foley's searching the missing person's database as we speak."

The edges of her mouth curl up in a grin. It throws me off. What's she up to? I watch as she saunters over to the coffee table, and roots inside her purse. She pulls out a pack of cigarettes and taps one out.

"You smoke?"

"Just now and then."

She lights up, inhales and blows out a stream, and then it hits me. A younger Mama. That's it. Rachel reminds me of what my mother must have been in her prime.

She ain't nothing like me, boy.

She takes another drag and squints at me through the smoke. "I might not be a legal professional, but I do have some information you don't. I found Dani."

I sit straight up. This back-and-forth game we play isn't what I hoped for tonight, but invigorating, nonetheless. "I'm all ears. Tell me."

She slips the ash-laden cigarette into a half-full bottle of beer. It fizzles, and acrid smoke clouds the bottle and puffs into the air. "Sorry. It's a nasty habit. Marco hates it. I've been trying to quit."

Enough about Marco. I really don't like the guy. "What about Dani White Elk?"

She sighs. "Dani and Kerry were both outsiders. Kerry because of her raising, and . . . well, Dani because of hers, too. Her family was from the reservation."

She lets that hang between us for a few beats, waiting, I suppose, for me to comment. I don't, and she continues. "Anyway, they worked together at the diner. They were good friends. She was possibly the only friend Kerry had."

"What about that night? Did she remember anything?"

"I talked to her about the photo with Kerry at the table that night of the party, the one I showed you. She remembered the conversation they had. She said that Kerry was upset with

Lucas. That she'd always known that he was a drinker but that she'd recently found out he'd been sleeping around. Kerry was so upset because it had been going on the whole time they were married."

I consider what she's saying. Lucas had some sort of affair, she found out about it, and confronted him. That explained the argument witnesses say they had that night. But the finger in the car she was driving? It was the one wild card in the whole scenario. Maybe if the finger was wrapped in a rag, or thrown under the seat, but in a shopping bag? Lucas didn't seem like the shopping type. But he did seem like the affair type. "I wonder if Lucas had some sort of sex-addiction problem, if that's why he cheated on his wife," I finally say. "Most serial killers do have some sort of sexual compulsion. It's what motivates them. They get off on the power they have over women. Killing becomes part of their foreplay. A sick game they play, over and over. I reach out, beckoning her back to the sofa.

You're playing a sick game now, boy.

She stays put. "You're right. It wasn't just one woman, but several."

I raise my brows.

"And there's more," she teases. "Dani told me something really interesting. Kerry said that one of the women was Abby Marshal."

The name zips through me like shock from a hot wire. "She was one of the victims."

"Yep."

"This is big."

She smirks.

"Did Dani say how Kerry found out about Lucas and Abby?"

"Wyatt told her."

Strange Murders: *"The Hatchet Killer"*
Transcript of the original episode, four years ago

Interview with Trevor Hunt, owner and pilot with Big Bear Air: We run a small two-chopper search and rescue unit out of Libby and work in cooperation with local and state law enforcement. We hold a 24/7 alert. The call came in from Lewis County Sheriff's Department at approximately 0700 hours with a mission to search and locate a fugitive at large, suspected to be in the Eastern region of the Kootenai. Both Bell B429 Global Ranger units took to the air immediately and conducted a forty-eight-hour coordinated search, which included the use of an MX-10 camera system, IR, laser designators, and night vision capabilities. We came up empty.

TWENTY-SIX

Kerry Grey

It's daybreak when I finally approach the house. I've walked all night, hiding in the brush, evading air search by crawling in mud and hiding in crevices and caves like a snake. I'm exhausted, broken, weak. I need a place to crash for a while, to rest and get my strength back. Then I plan to go back to get Joey and leave the area forever.

I look over the patchy yard, the giant satellite dish with rust streaks, and Dani's Ford Taurus, circa 1990 sometime, with equal amounts of rust. She still lives in her family home, about three miles from our place. It's isolated, on a poor piece of land, no views, just a dirt road and a smelly leach field. Dani answers on the second knock. Her eyes pop, and her thin lips gape open before she can recover.

"Hey Dani." Her straight hair is shorter than I remember and cut to accent her high cheekbones, but other than that, she looks the same.

"Kerry? What are you doing—"

"I'm in trouble. I need your help." The television is going in the background, and I hear my name on the newscast. "That stuff on the news . . . what they're saying about me, it's a lie. You know me. We're friends. You know it's not true. I've been framed. Again."

She stares at me, her eyes wide, her face tinged a sickly green color under her normally warm Native complexion. *She's scared of me?*

I offer a weak smile. "Wyatt and I went looking for Lucas . . . and things went wrong . . . I've been walking all night to get here. Please let me in."

"What do you mean? Why? What's happened to you?"

"I . . . I found Lucas."

She flinches. Her gaze darts to the surrounding woods. "He's here with you?"

"No. People have been wrong about him all these years. I was wrong. He never killed those women. He's not the Hatchet Killer."

"He's not? But . . ."

Confusion now mingles with her fear. I've probably said too much already. I shift. "Look. The police are watching our place, and they're looking for me. I didn't do anything, I swear. Everything you're hearing on the news is a lie. We're friends, right? You know me. You know I'm not a killer."

"Where's Wyatt? You said he went looking for Lucas with you." Gone is the fear as she blinks with incomprehension, her hand on the door sliding down slightly as if she doesn't have a good grasp on anything at the moment.

I hesitate. I can't answer that. I can't tell her that he's dead. That I *am* a killer and that I killed him. In self-defense, but still . . . I can hardly face the truth myself. "I know it's hard to believe, but Wyatt isn't who we thought he was. I don't want to believe it, but I think . . . that *he* killed those women, not Lucas. Wyatt is the Hatchet Killer." I chuckle tightly, but it comes out garbled. "Sorry. It just sounds so crazy, but remember that night? He was there. He must have planted that finger to frame Lucas so that he could have me for himself. I know how that sounds, but he was obsessed with me. You remember that, right? So, I think that's what happened, that he planted the finger, but when I stormed out of the party and took Lucas's car, his plan backfired. Think about Wyatt's childhood, his mother, his fixation on me."

Her fingers grip the door tight again. She shakes her head. "You're not making sense. You need to take all this to the police. I don't know how I can help—"

"I can't go to the police! Don't you understand? I'm an ex-con. They'll send me back to prison before they even listen to my story. You and I, we were never given half a chance, ever." I calm myself, get my voice under control, and put my hand on the door frame, sliding one foot closer to the inside. "It is just that I need a place to stay. For a couple days, that's all, until I can get Joey and then I'll leave. I'm going up north, across the border, but I won't leave Joey. I can't. You understand, don't you?"

She nods and swallows hard, opening the door wider.

I step inside. "Thank you."

She points a shaky finger at my blood-soaked shirt. "You're bleeding."

"Just a cut."

"Come on." She starts toward the back of the house, and I follow her to a small bathroom. I sit on the edge of the toilet lid while she digs through the cabinet under the sink. She pulls out a bottle of peroxide and a bag of cotton balls, some gauze and tape. "Get showered and clean your wound. Extra towels are in the cabinet. Shampoo and everything's in the shower. I'll set some clean clothes outside the door for you."

"Thank you." She won't look at me. After all these years, I've showed up on her doorstep, asking her to break the law for me. She's angry, I get it.

"I'll make you something to eat," she adds. "Then we can talk about this."

* * *

I take a long shower, hot water pouring over my sore muscles and my wound, washing off the sweat and stink of the last few days. Then I patch the gash in my arm and find the bundle of clothes outside the door. Jeans, a tank, black sweatshirt, socks, even panties and a bra. The jeans are loose on me, and so is the bra, but it feels good to wear something clean.

The newscast is still going in the kitchen. The anchor woman talks about my connection to Lucas and my current release from prison. The screen flashes to my old mugshot photo and a plea for viewers' assistance in finding me.

I turn away and go to the window. I squint down the lane, see nothing, and shake off an uneasy feeling. "I'm living in a nightmare. And it never stops," I say. But for the moment I can relax. Dani and I go way back. I can trust her, talk to her. I need to talk to someone.

"Sit down," she says. "Get something in your stomach. It'll help. Something hot in the belly always helps." She slides a plate of scrambled eggs in front of me and a mug of coffee, and then busies herself scrubbing the egg pan.

I gulp the coffee and it burns its way to my stomach, feels instantly warm and good. My muscles relax. I dig into the eggs. "I know it's hard to believe about Wyatt," I say between bites. "All these years everyone thought Lucas was the killer, but we were all fooled. Me especially. I just never would have . . ." She's turned off the water and is quiet. I look up and see her gaze fixed on something behind me.

"Dani, what is it?" My skin crawls. I sense something, or hear something maybe, and turn slightly.

Foley stands there, his gun pointed at me. Then two other officers appear with their guns drawn. I turn back to Dani, but she's disappeared. "You betrayed me!" I yell. My voice echoes through the kitchen. "I thought you were my friend!"

"Kerry Grey, you're under arrest." I hear Foley's voice behind me, a mixed bag of fear and excitement. I've been the object of his dreams for years now, ever since the first time he arrested me. I remember how his clammy hands felt on my skin then, wonder if I should just cash it all in, go for it, let them shoot me and spare myself the misery of going back to prison. Then I think of Joey.

"Don't make this hard on yourself." Foley again.

I slowly turn back and meet his gaze.

"Think of Joey," he says. "Do what's right for the boy."

Joey. I need to be there when they tell him his father is dead.

"Get up slowly and keep your hands where I can see them."

Joey, Joey, Joey . . . I rise and hold out my hands. Cold metal cuffs are slapped on my wrists. I'm dragged to the ground and pushed face down against the tile while hands grope at me and suddenly . . .

I'm back in prison, on work detail, laundry, it's not so bad, quiet work, then a noise from behind. I whip around, knuckles crash down on my face, heat slices through my gum as a tooth rips from its socket, I fall to the floor, coppery blood swirls over my tongue. I try to get up, but the floor is slick with blood, my blood, and hands are all over me, my jump suit is torn, fingernails claw at my face . . . I won't cry, I won't.

A sharp pain brings me back to reality. I've bitten through the inside of my cheek. Foley's talking to me, "Where's Lucas? You know where he is, tell me."

Blood fills my mouth, and then I'm jerked upward, on my feet. Foley leans in close, his breath smells of coffee and onion. "Who'd he hack up this time, huh?"

I gag on my own bloody spit. *I won't cry. I won't.*

He jerks me again and hot pain shoots through the base of my skull. "Whose body is it out there in my woods?"

I manage to lift my head and make eye contact with Foley.

His gaze is greedy. "I don't know anything about the body, I swear, but I know where Lucas is. I'll tell you where to find him, but only if you let me talk to Joey."

~ PART III ~

A NEW EPISODE

Strange Murders: *"Return of The Hatchet Killer"*
(Currently in production)

Welcome to tonight's episode of Strange Murders, *"The Hatchet Killer Returns." Four years ago, the nation was captivated by the gruesome murders of the three young women portrayed in* Strange Murders. *To-date, the mysterious case of the Hatchet Killer remains unsolved and the prime suspect, Lucas Yates, is still at large. In tonight's episode, we reveal that he may have struck again. Recently, another victim has fallen to what appears to be a hatchet killing. So, we've retuned to Joy, Montana, which once again finds itself in the epicenter of these heinous crimes, to provide viewers with a follow-up to the original case. There are still plenty of questions that need to be answered, like why did so much time elapse between the original three murders and this most recent killing? And what clues still lurk—along with Lucas Yates—in the deep woods of Montana? So listen closely—authorities may need your help to put to rest this long-standing case of the Hatchet Killer.*

TWENTY-SEVEN

Adam Nash

A woman's voice screams over the phone.

I blink as my mind scrabbles from the depths of sleep. *Miranda?* I sit up, push off the sheets, and grip the phone tighter. My wife's face flashes through my mind: perfectly pouty lips, blue eyes, and the parallel creases between her brows. My heart races, I break out in a sweat, and then the fog of sleep lifts and I know it's not Miranda. "Amber? What the hell?"

"He's dead. Dead."

I slip out of bed, step into my jeans, pulling at them while I balance my cell between my shoulder and chin. "Slow down. Who's dead?" I glance at the alarm clock on my bedside table. A little after 6:00 a.m. Rachel left in a huff a couple hours ago, leaving me in a haze of frustration.

"Hendricks. He . . . he—"

"Hendricks is dead?"

More babbling over the phone from Amber. She's incomprehensible.

"Take a deep breath and calm down, okay? Are you in danger?"

"No . . . he's . . . he's in his cell." More sobs, but I don't need her to explain anymore. I know what has probably happened.

"Okay, Amber. Listen. Is anyone else there with you? Are

you alone?" I'm trying to think through our shifts. We'd have two guys on patrol through the night, but Amber is the first one to arrive in the morning. She usually works 6:00 a.m. to 2:00 p.m. Foley and the others, me included, don't really get in until around 8:00 a.m. She would have been the first one downstairs in the basement. Probably taking Hendricks his breakfast. "Did you call for an ambulance?"

"No. He's dead. Really dead."

"I understand. But call for an ambulance anyway. Did you call Foley?"

"Yeah, but he didn't answer. I can't reach him, not even through the system."

"You mean he's on a call?" Was he at Wyatt's place?

I pull on pants, swish some mouthwash, spit, and head downstairs to look for my car keys.

"I don't know. I can't get anyone. Foley, Bird, McCulley. No one's answering."

I flip my cell over and check my display. Nothing. Where are they? My brain buzzes with possibilities. Did they find Lucas? One of the search team members might have called Foley directly. "It's okay. I'm on my way. Call for an ambulance and keep trying to reach Foley."

Hendricks is face down on the cell floor, the bunk is covered in excrement, a foul stench permeates the air, a take-out bag is by his bunk, a bag of chips open and strewn across the bare floor, a soda cup by his outstretched arm . . . I take in the whole scene in the span of a few seconds and then my stomach heaves. I turn to head back outside for fresh air, but McCulley intercepts me. He must have arrived after Amber called me. He looks relieved to see me. "Nash."

I swallow hard.

"How'd you know?" he asks.

"Amber called me. I got here as fast as I could. What happened?"

"No idea." He points to the EMTs huddled across the room. "They went in and checked. He's long gone. Foley's given orders that we're to stay out of the cell until the coroner gets here. Protocol. An outside agency will have to . . ." He raked his hand through his hair. "There will be an investigation."

I look over my shoulder and lower my voice. "How's she doing?"

McCulley's gaze slides to where Amber sits, slumped over my desk, crying into her hands. "Not good."

I nod. "I think she knew him personally."

McCulley's brows shoot up. "She did?"

"Yeah. I think she mentioned something about it. I might be wrong."

"Huh. Hendricks say anything to you yesterday?"

"No. Not really, other than ranting. He was angry, mostly. Wanted a lawyer. His hearing had just been set, so . . . uh . . ." I don't hear Amber anymore, but I keep my voice low. "Uh . . . he seemed okay, you know, and now . . . I just can't believe it."

"I feel bad about this, too, but don't beat yourself up over it, you've got to stay focused. Especially now."

"Why? What do you mean?"

"We just arrested Kerry Yates."

"What? When?"

"Maybe thirty minutes ago. Foley and Bird are bringing her in now. We heard the ambulance dispatch over the two-way, so Foley sent me ahead to get this situation under control."

"Why didn't someone call me about Kerry?"

"Hadn't had a chance. I'm letting you know now."

"Yeah, yeah, sure. Sorry. Where'd you find her?"

"She'd shown up at a friend's house. The friend called us."

"Wyatt Jones's place?"

"Wyatt's? No, Dani White Elk's."

Foley comes down the steps, pauses and says something to the EMTs and glances inside the cell before coming our way.

"You've got Kerry?" I ask.

He holds up his hands. "Hold on." He walks past us to Amber. I watch as he talks to her. She wipes her eyes and sniffles, pointing toward the cell as she speaks. After a while, he stands and pats her on the shoulder, then comes back to us. "What can you tell me about this?" he asks me.

"Nothing really. He was fine when I left yesterday."

"Anybody been in that cell?"

"Just the paramedics," McCulley says.

He looks at me. "Where'd he get the food?"

"I guess from Amber. I remember her ordering from The Gold Bar yesterday."

"You check it over before she gave it to him?"

"No."

He looks at McCulley.

"She must've had Bird take care of it," he says. "I'll check with him."

Foley shakes his head. "All this because the guy couldn't make his damn parole meetings and ended up here. Senseless."

We all stare at our feet.

"This is a problem," Foley finally says. "We're waiting on the agency people from Helena to get here. They'll want to review camera footage, interview everyone . . . all that's going take a while. We'll transfer the Yates woman to the county facility in Libby. It's probably better to hold her down there anyway. McCulley, stay here and keep things secure. And tell Amber to see what she can find out about Hendrick's family. Nash, you come with me."

"To interview Kerry?" I ask, my question too quick, voice too anxious. I try to look casual and fail.

Foley smiles as he replies, "Yeah. She's prepared to tell us where Lucas is hiding."

Mama's voice now, also quick and too anxious: *This is it, boy. This is our big chance.*

Strange Murders: *"Return of The Hatchet Killer"*
(Currently in production)

Unedited interview with Angela Turner, mother of missing hiker, Allison Turner: It's been a nightmare that no parent should have to endure. Our Allison was a college student, and she came up here hiking with her boyfriend. We didn't hear from her for a couple of days, but we figured she was out of cell range. Then we got a call from her boyfriend, saying that he had been injured, she went for help and disappeared. Well, we came straight here. The sheriff's department, all the agencies involved, were wonderful to us. We joined in the search, of course, but after a few days . . . (soft crying) Excuse me. After a few days of not finding her, we were giving up hope. Then they found the remains in the woods near where Allison would have been hiking and we thought . . . (more crying) I just can't tell you how horrible it was. To think that your daughter might have fallen into the hands of a psychotic killer. Everyone kept saying it looked like the Hatchet Killer. Then, thank God, our Allison turned up. She was okay. Alive! I've never been so grateful in my whole life. My husband and I want to personally thank all those who joined the search effort for Allison, especially Sheriff Foley and his deputies who worked tirelessly to support us during this difficult time. And I want to add, to those parents before us, who lost their daughters in such a violent way, I am truly sorry. And to the current victim, and her family, our hearts and prayers go out to you.

TWENTY-EIGHT

Kerry Grey

My left hand is cuffed to a table inside a dull, narrow room where the most interesting thing is the round framed clock clicking off seconds, *click, click* . . . It's been over an hour since Foley and his deputy dragged me down Main Street, past an *Strange Murders* film crew and chanting bystanders and shuffled me into this dismal room.

Desperation twists in my belly. *I can't go back to prison. I can't.* I lean forward, close my eyes, and imagine being on the mountain, on my front porch, the stars, a light breeze, the sound of a hoot owl. Pops is inside tinkering around with this and that, and Joey is safely tucked in bed, asleep. The world is right, my anxiety calms and my muscles loosen, and I drift into sleep until the sound of the door pulls me back to reality.

"Your PO is here." It's Foley. He's followed into the room by Nash who takes the chair to my right and stares at me with sorrowful eyes. *Spare me the pity, Nash.* Foley sits directly across from us. He looks flushed, like his heart is beating too fast. He points to a camera mounted on the wall and looks down at a notebook, his chin disappearing into the fat folds on his neck.

"This is an official interview and it's being recorded. For the record, I'm Sheriff Foley. I'm here with Parole Officer Adam Nash."

I glare at Nash. I used to like him. Thought he might help me, but I should've known better. No cop has ever helped me.

Foley continues, "First, for the record, please state your full name and birthdate."

I sit back, stare hard for a few beats, and then mumble off my information. Foley reads me my rights; we all sign a piece of paper, and then I wait until Foley clears his throat. "We picked you up at Dani White Elk's residence, correct?"

I shrug. "You were there."

"This is for the record. So yes, or no."

"Yes."

"Where were you before that?"

"Out and about."

"Can you be more specific."

I sigh. *This is going to take all day.* "I went after Lucas because I was afraid for my son. He's been watching our place, trying to lure Joey away. I talked to Nash about it."

Foley glances at Nash and then narrows his eyes my way. "One of the hatchets we took from your barn came back with blood on it."

My back goes rigid. "I'm being framed again."

"How so?"

"The hatchet was planted. I'm sure of it. There was someone at our place the other night. We think he was in the barn."

"Lucas?"

"That's what I thought at the time."

"What do you mean?"

"I mean, I know who planted the hatchet and it wasn't Lucas."

A beat and a half of silence later, Foley asks, "Who was it?"

"I'll tell you after I see my son."

"We'll get to that, but first—"

"No. Nothing until I talk to Joey."

"The deal is that you see your son in exchange for telling us where Lucas is hiding. I haven't asked you that yet. I'm asking about the hatchet in your barn."

"I want to see my son."

"And you will. I promise. You'll see him. But you'll have to give me something to go on here."

"Okay. I'll give you something. We've all been wrong about Lucas. All this time . . . it's crazy, but now I know. It wasn't Lucas who killed those women, it was Wyatt Jones."

Foley flinches. Nash leans forward. "Do you have proof of this?" he asks.

"He's not who you think he is. He's like one of those serial killers that no one would ever suspect, but I know him. His mother was a . . . she was horrible to him. He had a difficult childhood. She was verbally abusive. It affected him. Even as a kid, he was different. And he was obsessed with me. He used to follow me places. He followed me that night to The Gold Bar. He probably planted the bag with the finger in Lucas's car, thinking he was going to frame Lucas and have me to himself."

Foley's eyes grow small. "You're making this up. Wyatt Jones is—"

"No, he's not what you think. He's a killer."

Foley turns his palms up. "Where's the proof?"

I clamp my mouth shut.

He chuckles. "So, you don't have proof. You just *feel* like it was Wyatt who killed those women, not Lucas?"

"It's your job to find proof, not mine."

His expression turns dark, and the room falls silent. I shift, trying to change positions, my shoulder hurts, my face hurts where I was punched, and now my armpit as well from where Foley manhandled me.

"Can we take the cuff off?" Nash asks.

Foley glares at him and scribbles something in his notebook.

Finally, he says to me, "So you found Lucas? Where is he?"

My neck crackles as I rotate it. Why won't they just let me see Joey? "Yeah, I found him. I knew where to look."

"You knew where to look? How long have you known his location? He's a wanted felon. Are you aware that it's a crime to withhold—"

"Why would I trust you? You'd already made up your mind about me." I hesitate and then give up a little more information. "Lucas left something in the treehouse that told me where I could find him."

They wait.

I look away. "I'm not saying nothing else until I see Joey."

Foley doesn't give up. "Tell me what he left."

I fold my arms.

We wait it out a few more seconds until Foley tosses down his pen and pulls out his cell phone. "Bird. Ride out to the Grey's cabin and pick up Callan and the kid. Bring them in here . . . yes, right now."

Strange Murders: *"Return of the Hatchet Killer"*
(Currently in production)

Camera footage: The interior of The Gold Bar
Unedited interview with Brax Ryan, founder of The Hatchet Club: I started the club right after the first murders occurred. The entire community was in a state of panic. We had three dead women, slain in the most brutal manner imaginable, all within a fairly short period of time, and the killer still on the loose. Joy used to be a thriving town, but when news that we had a murderer lurking in the woods got out, tourism fell off. Businesses suffered. People left. No one knew who the Hatchet Killer's next victim might be. Our members come from all walks of life, doctors, nurses, housewives, all dedicated to finding Lucas Yates, bringing justice to the victim's families, and restoring the reputation of our town. We've worked diligently over the past four years, dedicating all our free time to the cause. Then we have this new murder. If the sheriff had done his job, had located that killer at any point in the last four years, another poor woman wouldn't have become a victim. I'm not saying the deputies didn't try, but it is clear they didn't try hard enough. So, when they call us a vigilante group or activists, I say, you bet we are! Someone has to stop these killings. With this new murder, we've doubled down our efforts. I even approached Kerry Grey, Lucas Yates's wife, asking for her help, which she refused. Despite this, I'm proud to say we've managed to document several sightings of Lucas Yates. Yes, we've seen him. And I believe we were this close (hand gesture) to finding him before the local authorities shut our operation down.

TWENTY-NINE

Adam Nash

"There's evidence that supports her story," I tell Foley, but he's only half-listening. He's got a forest service map unfolded over his desk and is scanning everything within a twenty-mile radius of the Grey's property.

I continue. "The photos I found at Wyatt's place. Hundreds of photos of Kerry. Obsessive isn't even a strong enough word for it. He'd been stalking her before she went to prison."

Foley responds without looking up. "She knew where Lucas was hiding because of something he left behind for the kid. You heard her say that, right?"

"Yeah. So?"

"When we arrested her, she had a piece of gold in her pocket. A nugget. Good sized, too.

Odd, don't you think?"

"Yeah, but what's that have to do—"

"It's worth more money than those folks usually see." He traces his finger over the map, then taps a spot. "There are a few marked claims out by their place, and—"

"Did you hear me? Wyatt was stalking her. And I haven't had a chance to tell you, but my neighbor, her name is Rachel. Rachel Santini, she—"

"I don't have time to hear about neighborhood gossip."

"This isn't gossip. She has photos from that night at the party. Wyatt is in one. But when he was interviewed for *Strange Murders*, he lied. Said he wasn't at the party."

Foley waved it off. "It was national television. He may not have wanted it known that he was at a party with a serial killer. I wouldn't."

"I'm just saying that we should look closer at the guy. See what we can find out about him. There's something else, too." I told him about Lucas and Abby Marshal having an affair. "Wyatt told Kerry the night of the party at The Gold Bar."

Foley frowned. "Doesn't change much. Only makes Lucas seem more guilty. I've known Wyatt since he was a kid. Known his whole family. It's not him. She's putting up some sort of smoke screen. You can't trust that woman." The map curls as he lifts his coffee mug from the corner and takes a sip. "That chunk of gold has something to do with Lucas's location, I just can't figure it out. Doesn't matter. She'll talk as soon as the boy gets here."

I remember the last promise he made and broke to Joey. "You're going to make good on your end of the deal, right? You said—"

"I know what I said."

He's pissed now. Foley doesn't like people stepping on his toes.

"This Hendricks deal changes things," Foley says. "As soon as we get everything we can, you and McCulley can transport her down to the county jail in Libby. Probably better to get her off our hands anyway, with that film crew hanging around, and those Hatchet Club people protesting. Now, is there anything else?"

He goes back to studying the map. I stare at the bald spot on his head for a few seconds before leaving to look for Amber.

I find her behind the front counter. Her eyes are swollen,

her lips puffy. She breaks down as soon as she sees me. "They're asking so many questions about Hendricks. Why do you think they're doing that? Am I a suspect?"

"It's their job, that's all."

"How did this happen?" Her voice cracks. "He was fine yesterday." She opens her desk drawer and roots for something.

"I don't know. I really don't. It could be anything. Don't get all worked up over it, okay? You'll be fine."

"But . . ." She slams the drawer shut and breaks into a fresh round of sobs.

"Stop this. Try to focus. There's a lot going on here and you have a job to do."

She blows her nose and nods.

"I saw a camera crew outside earlier," I say.

"Those *Strange Murders* people. They've interviewed about everyone in town already. Don't get any ideas about talking to them. Foley's orders. Not a word about anything. We're supposed to avoid them."

"Kinda hard to do."

"Yeah." Her face drains. She dabs at her mascara smudges. "Do you think I'm going to lose my job. They've been asking how well I knew Hendricks. Do they think I had something to do with his death?"

I hold up my finger. "Hey now. You know as well as I do that Hendricks was a heavy drug user. That's what landed him in prison in the first place. And by the looks of things out at his place, I pretty much guarantee that he was using again, which is probably why he was skipping his parole meetings. A guy like that, it's just a matter of time. So don't worry about all their questions. They're just doing their job. After the autopsy, they'll have all the answers they need, and things will get back to normal before you know it."

She blows out a long breath. "Sure. Well, at least we've got

Kerry behind bars. Was it her? Did she help Lucas chop up that poor woman they found?"

"You know I can't talk about that."

She looks hurt and hunches in on herself, Liberty deflating to what looks like a crumpled butterfly. A twinge of guilt flashes through me. I should do something to comfort her, but before I even move, she must sense it, like a predator senses a vulnerable spot suddenly exposed. She straightens her shoulders and meets my gaze, her bloodshot eyes hopeful. "Hey, is Miranda still off pouting somewhere? I mean, if she's gone, maybe we could get some dinner together, or something."

My gut turns sour. I think of Miranda and her schedules, and Rachel, the way she teases me, and now Amber, always begging. A bile-like taste creeps up the back of my throat. "I don't think so, Amber. Not tonight, okay?" Not ever.

A half hour later, Callan and Joey are brought in. Callan looks sullen and drawn. Aged. And gone is Joey's usual look of defiance. In its place is something that looks like sadness, or perhaps vulnerability. I feel my chin quivering and I quickly turn away.

Foley ushers them down the hall, parking them near the door to the interrogation room. "I'll tell you when you can come in," he says. Then to me, "Come on, Nash. You ready?"

I catch up, and he grips the map in one hand and opens the door with the other, wide enough that Kerry can see her grandfather and son standing there.

"Joey. Joey," she cries out, straining at her cuff, reminding me of that day out at their place when their dog kept snarling and pulling against his yard chain.

Foley shuts the door behind us.

"Bring Joey to me. Please." Kerry's voice is tiny, like a young girl.

Foley remains standing, folding his arms across his chest,

the forest service map rolled against his armpit. "I need to know where Lucas is first."

I look between Foley and Kerry. I'm not sure what to do with myself. This whole thing feels off. It's not what I expected, or maybe it is, and I didn't want to believe it was going to unfold this way. I want to tell Kerry to keep her mouth shut, that Foley is going to screw her over.

She tenses. "You said that—"

"You're not in a position to negotiate. Give me Lucas's location."

She stares at the door as if she can see through it.

Don't trust him, Kerry. Don't trust him.

Foley presses her. "Why are you protecting him? Tell me where he is." He lays out the map. "Better yet, show me."

She looks down and traces a shaky finger along the map, stopping at a certain point. "He's here. On the north side of the creek, up in the hills. If you people know anything about tracking, you should find him."

Foley straightens, a smile turning at the edge of his lips.

"He's dead. And so is Wyatt." She takes a deep breath and spills everything, telling us about how she and Wyatt had gone searching for Lucas, Wyatt's injury, or so she thought, Lucas's final words before Wyatt shot him in cold blood, and then turned the gun on her. "We struggled and Wyatt fell, hit his head. I was defending myself. Not that I expect you to believe me. You never have."

Foley says nothing for a long while. Then Kerry asks, "Can I see my son now?"

I head to the door, ready to let both Callan and Joey into the room. I reach for the knob and pop open the door, but Foley slams his hand on the table. "Leave them where they are."

Kerry squeezes her eyes shut and whimpers. I step into the hall, closing the door behind me. I can't watch this. The air fills with Kerry's shrill screams and the sound of metal clinking as she jerks on her restraints. Joey stares at the door wide-eyed, his face pale. Callan wraps a protective arm around his shoulder.

"I'm sorry," I whisper and turn away. I hear Foley come into the hall and murmur something to Callan. Then he calls after me, "Nash!"

I keep walking.

"Nash, stop right there."

I whip around. "You lied to her. She held up her end of the bargain. You told her she could talk to her son."

"And she will. Eventually."

"That's not what you led her to believe."

Foley's face reddens, and he steps within an arm's length of me, his lips curling with each word. "What do we know about what she's telling us. Nothing. For all we know, Lucas is out there with other women's hacked-up bodies, or God knows what, and that woman in there knows. How's it going to look if I kowtowed to the Hatchet Killer and his accomplice. No, she ain't getting nothing until I know what's going on here. And don't you forget, we still have an unidentified victim. I may still need the kid as leverage." He poked his finger at my chest. "Those Hatchet Club people are out there, just waiting for me to screw up, and it's not going to happen this time. I am not about to be made a fool of again. Now watch your mouth and go round up McCulley and you two get that Yates woman down to Libby and properly locked up."

Strange Murders: *"Return of the Hatchet Killer"*
(Currently in production)

Unedited interview with Chrissie VanElst, Kerry Grey's former classmate: I'd always had my suspicions about Kerry. People thought she was strong and independent, and antisocial. And she was all that on the outside, but I think there was something deep inside her that longed for other people's approval. I'd seen it back in school, times where she tried hard to fit in with the rest of us, but just couldn't manage to break through her social barriers. It's sad, really. How someone like that can fall into the trap of going along with about anything. I can see how Lucas would have been able to convince her into going along with killing those women.

THIRTY

Adam Nash

An insect hits the windshield in front of me and leaves a smear of blood and wings and some brown goop. "Hit the wipers, would ya?" I say to McCulley.

We're halfway to Libby, Kerry cuffed and in the back of the cruiser, McCulley driving. He has a stain on his right shirtsleeve where an overdramatic protestor chucked a Big Gulp pop at him as we escorted Kerry out of the building earlier. More like bum-rushed her out, elbowing past the *Strange Murders* camera crew as they scurried up to us, shouting questions, flailing a microphone our way. Rachel, too, frantic and crazed, edged into the crowd, her wide eyes on Kerry, not seeing me, or so it seemed. Kerry's arrest has made everyone in town half-insane.

McCulley flips on the wipers, and they smear a rainbow of bug guts over my side of the windshield. I raise my hands in frustration and look at McCulley. He shrugs. "I'm out of wiper fluid," he explains.

I work my jaw and glance over my shoulder at Kerry. She avoids eye contact. Back at the department she'd been hysterical, calling out for her son. Now she's eerily quiet, as if prison cell doors have already shut her out. Maybe they have.

I turn back and close my eyes, witnessing the same scene over and over: Kerry in the interrogation room hunched over with despair; then the spark of hope, her stepping out in faith to trust; followed by the pained anguish in her voice as she realized that Foley had betrayed her and kept her from Joey. All because Foley failed years ago, and now he is punishing Kerry for his past inadequacy. I'm pissed at Foley for the way he's treated all of the Grey family.

"We might have a problem," McCulley says.

I open my eyes and sit straighter. "What?"

"Check out the vehicle coming up behind us."

My side mirror shows a dark SUV bearing down on us from behind. McCulley speeds up, and I pull the handheld radio and call it in. "Amber. Nash. We need back-up. En route, mile marker—"

I'm pressed back in the seat as McCulley accelerates.

"They're right on us!" he calls out.

"Amber, we're being pursued. Black Suburban, license plate . . ." But I can't see the plate. The vehicle is next to us now, windows down, people hanging out and screaming at us. Hatchet Club people, that kid Brax, he's leaning out the window, something is in his hand, and it's pointed at us. They're dangerously close— "Watch out!"

McCulley swerves, and the cruiser slides out of control. Kerry screams, I cover my head and brace myself, tires squeal, the Suburban spins toward us—*crunch!*—we jolt forward, my belt clotheslines my chest, the airbag smashes my face, and my nostrils flatten. McCulley's scream reverberates through the car as it flips: trees, sky, trees, sky, a flash of brown bark, and with a loud *thud,* glass crackles—and we jerk to a sudden halt.

The world goes silent as if all life has exhaled.

I'm stunned, my breath gone, and then from behind me, a small groan, and the faint sound of glass being scraped away, something sliding . . . and I know that Kerry is escaping. I gasp for a lungful of air, push back from the airbag, my face on fire, one eye sticky and swollen shut. Next to me, I see McCulley is unconscious but breathing. I snap off my seatbelt and whip around.

Kerry is gone.

My hand trembles as I call for help and then reach under the dash. I hit the button to unlatch the shotgun.

Strange Murder: *"Return of the Hatchet Killer"*
(Currently in production)

Unedited Interview with Rachel Santini, certified counselor, Hatchet Club member, and true crime enthusiast: I've dedicated my career to helping spouses resolve marital issues and improve their love lives. Perhaps that's why this case fascinates me. So much of what has happened during the investigation of this case revolves around Lucas and Kerry's relationship. In my experience, what happens outside a marriage is often the result of dissatisfaction or unresolved conflicts within the relationship. I've helped numerous couples recognize that. So, what underlying issue in his marriage drove Lucas Yates to seek out single women and then savagely kill them? And what compelled Kerry to simply stand by complacently while he acted on his impulse to kill? Because in my opinion, it would be impossible for a wife to be completely ignorant of her husband's perversions or obsessions. If they had only sought out counseling for their marital problems, all this senseless killing would never have happened.

THIRTY-ONE

Kerry Grey

Nash is stirring, moaning, and making deep sucking noises, but the other deputy is slumped motionless against the deployed airbag. Maybe he's dead, I don't know. We were hit hard, flipped over, and slammed into a tree. Now the window next to me is cracked and partially cleared, and I've got an escape route. For a second, I hesitate. When I get caught, and I will, they'll tack on an escape charge, a felony. But what does it really matter? I'm going back to prison anyway, and I need to see Joey.

I undo my belt and push up on the seat, sliding my sleeve over my hand to clear out the rest of the glass shards still stuck in the frame. Nash is moving now; there's not much time. I hoist myself up and climb through the window, my right leg scraping against a missed piece of jagged glass. The shard digs into my skin, sending hot searing pain through my leg. My jeans wick the blood like an absorbent paper towel.

I clamor over the rocky ground to the other side of the car and work fast, yanking open the crumpled door, and pulling cuff keys from the small clip bag on the unconscious deputy's belt. I kneel, my blood-soaked jeans sticking to my legs, and twist my wrist to get at the cuff's keyhole. The metal rubs raw against my flesh and my fingers cramp as I try to manipulate the key into the lock. I miss and drop the key. My pulse races. I hear Nash moving in the car. I snatch up the key and try again. The cuffs finally pop open and fall to the ground. I run.

The road is empty, with no sign of the SUV that hit us, but then a small car rounds the curve and stops only feet from me. A young woman steps out, eyes wide. She looks at me, at the blood staining my jeans, and her hands fly to her face. "Oh . . . what happened? Are you okay?"

"An accident. Hit and run." I point to the partially visible crumpled police cruiser. "Two cops need help. Do you have a cell phone?" I step closer to her.

"Yeah. Yeah, hold on."

She turns, bends over and reaches back into her vehicle. I clench my fists, raise my hands, and come down hard on the back of her head. She crumples. I yank her out of the way and climb into her car, toss out her bag, cram the car into gear, and speed off.

For the first few miles, I check my mirror constantly, then turn off Highway 37 onto Pinkham Creek Road and then a national forest service road. I don't know where I am exactly, but I'm heading east. Home is east. Where Joey is.

I press the accelerator harder and the car rattles. The ruts are deep, carved by heavy logging equipment on wet roads, and it sounds like the undercarriage is being scraped away. The jarring ride shakes my brain and it hits me: *What have I done? That girl was still breathing, right? I didn't hit her that hard. Did I?* My hands shake, tears course down my face. *I only ever wanted to protect Joey, but Foley lied to me. Wyatt, Dani, Nash . . . all liars*—a hard *thump* gnashes my teeth, and I force away those thoughts and slow the car slightly. I'm determined to stay focused. The plan is to get as far as I can on the forest service roads, ditch the car, and go the rest of the way on foot.

I shake my head at the craziness of it, but why not? Just add assault and grand larceny to the charges, any of which will land me back in prison anyway, where I'll rot out the rest of my life.

But Joey . . . Sweat pours down my face, my palms are slick on the wheel. I grip it tighter. I need to be the one who tells him that his father is dead, not Foley or one of his minions. And I want him to know the truth, that his father was innocent, that he is not the son of a serial killer. Joey was right all along, and I need him to forgive me for not believing him. I think of Lucas on the cabin floor, bleeding out, his last words—words that proved his love for his son. And I think of Wyatt, the look in his eyes when he knew that I realized that he was the monster who everyone has feared all these years. Wyatt is the Hatchet Killer. Only no one believes me. Not that it matters.

It only matters that Joey hears the truth.

Strange Murders: *"Return of the Hatchet Killer"*
(Currently in production)

Unedited interview with Nettie Crane, long-time Joy resident: I've lived in Joy my whole life and I ain't never seen things this crazy, with all this protestin' and talk going round about that Hatchet Killer and his wife. Even heard someone sent a sawed-off leg in a box to the sheriff's department. Bet that set 'em thinking. Now, I'm not an official member of that club in town, but I've spent some time searchin' for Lucas out in the woods hoping to get myself a piece of that reward being offered. Even seen him up on Cutter's Ridge once, let me tell you. But he's a slippery one and I wasn't up to no hikin' that day, so I just let him go. But me and most everyone in town's been lookin' for him. It's just a matter of time before he's caught.

THIRTY-TWO

Adam Nash

I raise the shotgun and approach slowly. "Don't move, don't move." She doesn't and as I get closer, I see that it's not Kerry lying still in the road, but a girl, young, maybe sixteen, with dark hair, and a ghoulish looking face with pale skin and dark lipstick.

One of the Hatchet Club people? I glance up and down the empty road. The SUV is gone. Did they head out to chase down Kerry and leave one of their own behind?

I lower the gun and check for a pulse. The girl stirs and opens her eyes, startling at the sight of me. She sits up, winces and grabs the back of her neck.

"Try not to move," I say. "You've been in an accident. I'm with the sheriff's department. There's an ambulance on the way."

"Accident?"

"With Brax."

She glances at the wrecked cruiser and back to me. "Brax?"

She's confused. Dazed. Head injury probably. "The guy who was with you in the SUV."

A blank stare.

"You were in the black SUV that ran us off the road."

"No. No, I swear. My car is . . ." she looks around, her

kohl-darkened eyes puzzling over the empty roadway, "my car is gone. A woman asked for help, then . . . I think she hit me." She touches her neck again.

Kerry. "What's your car look like?"

"A blue Corolla. It's older, I can't even remember the year. Over ten years old. Will insurance cover it, do you think?"

"Stay here and don't move. You're going to need to be checked over." Another vehicle approaches, a Dodge Ram truck, and slows down, the driver gawking at the scene. I motion for him to stop, blocking any unwary traffic that might come upon the girl. I hear sirens in the distance. "Help is coming," I tell her, then head back to check on McCulley again. He's awake and in pain, his face cut up from the air bag. My foot bumps against something and I look down to see a pair of cuffs on the ground.

She's getting away, boy. You're letting her get away.

"You're going to be okay," I tell McCulley. "The ambulance is about here."

"The Yates woman? Is she dead?"

"No. Window blew out and she's gone. Hang tight, okay? I'm going after her."

I commandeer the truck from the bystander, a skinny bearded guy with hollowed out cheeks and a veiny nose, and take off heading east, the shotgun resting on the passenger seat. I phone Amber and give her my destination—Kerry Grey's cabin. Time is against me; she has a head start. But I know she'll be there. She won't leave the area without her son.

Strange Murders: *"Return of the Hatchet Killer"*
(Currently in production)

Unedited Interview with Trish Peterson: Kerry Grey's son is in school with my son, Aiden. They were in the same class together, that is, before I requested that Aiden be moved to a different homeroom. Can you blame me? Kerry Grey's boy had been acting out, becoming angry and aggressive toward other kids in school. It worried me. I mean, it's understandable that he would have some issues, considering that his father is a known serial killer. But I became especially concerned when he brought a small carving to school and told my son that it was a recent gift from his father, Lucas. It was a small bird carved out of bone. Animal, I thought, but now . . . I hope it wasn't from a bone belonging to some poor woman he killed. (shudders) I knew something bad was going to happen as soon as I heard Kerry Grey was coming home. Ask me, we'd all be safer with her back in prison.

THIRTY-THREE

Kerry Grey

I dump the car on a forest service road a mile from the house and walk the rest of the way. When I get to the cabin, I find Pops rocking on the porch. He looks up, sees me, and springs from the chair. "Kerry?" He looks at my leg and my face, which must be black and blue by now. "You've been hurt."

"It's okay, Pops. Don't worry. I'm okay. Just a cut and it's already stopped bleeding."

"But how'd you . . . did they let you go?"

"No. I escaped." I'm breathless, as much from facing Pops and Joey as from the pain throbbing through my leg.

He turns ashen.

"Sit back down," I tell him. "They'll come here looking for me soon, so there's not much time. I need to talk to you and Joey. Where is he?"

"He's out in the treehouse. Ran out there as soon as we got home."

I glance that way. *How much time do I have before they come for me?* "Lucas is dead, and I believe he was innocent." Pops opens his mouth but doesn't say anything. I tell him everything that happened in the woods. "Wyatt and I were fighting, and . . . and I pushed him. He hit his head. He was so still and there was blood, so much blood. I left him there. I ran. I had to. He aimed a gun at me and . . . he's dead."

"You killed him?" He clasps his head. "But . . . you had to defend yourself. It was self-defense."

"Yes, but who would believe it?"

He scrapes his hand through his hair, his jaw chewing over these revelations. "You should have stayed here like I told you, but you couldn't leave it alone, could you? Leave the past in the past, that's what I said, but you didn't listen and now—"

"Leave the past in . . .? And how would I do that when no one else around here will?" I stand and grasp the porch railing. "Listen, I love you, and maybe you're right, but I don't have time for this right now. And it doesn't really matter . . . I need to talk to Joey. I don't want him to hear about Lucas from someone else. And I want him to know the truth."

Pops sinks back and starts rocking again, staring out past me, into the yard and at the treehouse. "Did Wyatt confess?"

"No."

He frowns. "How do you know that you have the truth?"

"I don't know. Maybe no one knows the truth."

He stands and leans against the porch rail next to me. He's trembling. "After you tell Joey, then what? You going to run for it? Live your life looking over your shoulder? Take . . . take Joey with you?"

I turn and fall into his arms, pressing my head against his chest. The smell of wood, hard work, the wind, and his heartbeat, steady and strong, but his body feels thinner and frail, and I know the toll everything has taken on him. My mother's death, the trouble I caused growing up, the murders and the constant press surrounding our family. The one steady in his life has been Joey, and he's worried that I'm going to take him away.

Time. I'm running out of time.

"It's going to be okay. I promise, Pops." I pull back and stare into the face of the only person who loves me without question. The one person I have hurt the worst. And we both know nothing will ever be okay.

Joey is waiting for me. I feel his presence as I climb each rung of the ladder to the sawed-out door in the floorboards. He's in the corner, sitting with his knees pulled against his chest, his face blotchy. He unfolds himself and turns toward me.

"Joey, I have to talk to you about something important."

"I can't believe they let you go."

"They didn't. And I don't have much time. What I have to say is very important, do you understand?" I sit cross-legged on the floor near him. A slight breeze blows through the window, lifting his hair off his forehead. I resist the urge to touch it.

"You went lookin' for Dad so that you could kill him. I heard you talking to Pops before you left."

I take a few deep breaths. "I know what you heard. I know how it sounded . . . and you're right. I did want to kill him, but it was to protect you."

"Did you kill him?"

"No." Tears sting my eyes. He sees it and looks scared. I realize he's seldom seen me cry. "But your father is dead, Joey. I'm sorry. He's dead."

He flinches, his body trembling, but his expression frozen. The world goes silent. I see his pupils dilate until his eyes look like two black holes. "Joey," I whisper. "Joey." *Stay with me, son. Please. Stay with me.*

I scoot closer and take his hand. He doesn't pull away, but his skin is cold and sweaty at the same time. Outside, the silence is broken by the sound of a car coming down the drive. They're here for me. My heart sinks. I need more time. "You need to know he died trying to protect me from the real Hatchet Killer, Wyatt Jones. Your father wasn't a killer, he was a hero. One day, I'll tell you everything that happened, but for now I want you to remember what I've said. I want you to know that it's the truth. No matter what you hear on the news or from other people, know that what I've told you is the truth."

"Why should I believe you?"

"Because I've risked everything to come here to tell you this. I should have believed you about your father, but I didn't and I'm sorry. I owed it to you to come here . . . and to your dad." I reach up and clasp my hands on his cheeks and tip my head toward him, until our foreheads touch. Tears flow steady from my eyes now. "The last thing your father told me, the last words he spoke, was that he wanted you to know the truth. He loved you, Joey. He loved you."

A long, jagged breath escapes his lips, he presses closer to me, and his own tears begin to fall.

Strange Murders: *"Return of the Hatchet Killer"*
(Currently in production)

Unedited interview with Sheila Berg, MD, FAPA, Lewis County Mental Health Center (continued): It's often the case that after a killer is prosecuted and brought to justice, the family is left with unanswered emotional needs. Lucas and Kerry's son, for example. He faces multiple hardships, not only coming to terms with his father's crimes, but also his absence all these years, and the extent of his mother's involvement or complacency in the murders. He'll also be exposed to a toxic fame that will follow him his entire life. This family will need support and love from this community in order to recover from this trauma.

THIRTY-FOUR

Adam Nash

"I know she's here." I draw my weapon as I approach Callan. He's rocking on the front porch as if he hasn't a care in the world. "Did you hear me? I know she's here."

"You're right," he says.

My senses heighten, a high-pitched buzz rings in my ears. Is her gun trained on me right now?

"She's talking to the boy."

"Where? In the cabin?" My gaze whips to the cabin door, the windows, back to Callan.

"Give them a little time," he says.

"Where are they?"

He stares straight ahead, the porch boards squeaking beneath his rocker.

I know she's cornered and angry and I should wait for back-up. Several units were dispatched from the main department in Libby; they'll be here any minute. But a minute is long enough for her to slip away again, and for me to lose my chance.

I pass by Callan, open the door, and enter, my firearm trembling in my hand. I crouch by the door until my eyes adjust to the dim light, then scan my surroundings. The cabin is primitive and sparce, a couple chairs by a stone fireplace, a simple kitchen, a wood table. I cross the room and slowly open a closed door to find a small, tidy bedroom. Callan's room, probably. It's clear. Then, I turn and approach the loft ladder, my gun pointed upward as I climb to the loft where two doors, both closed, face one another, separated by a small sitting area with a window seat.

I call out, "Kerry, it's Adam Nash! I'm coming in. Don't try anything stupid." I listen intently for sounds from either room.

Nothing.

I go left first. Kerry's room, simple, yet feminine in its own way, and empty. Joey's room is next, and it's also empty. I lower the gun and sigh. Where are they? I move to the window, glance across the yard, to the woods, the chicken house, the barn, and . . . the treehouse.

By the time I get outside, she's already standing under the treehouse with Joey. As I draw closer and see that she doesn't have a weapon, I holster my gun. "Kerry. You'll have to come with me."

"I know."

"Step away from Joey and walk this way."

Joey's hand tightens on hers as she starts toward me. He begs, "Don't go. Don't go with him."

"I have to go."

He looks my way, and a sense of dread begins to swell in my stomach. Something isn't right. This is the kid who gave his mother up only a day ago. The kid who blamed her for losing his father. Tough and determined before, now I see a crack in his façade. A vulnerability in the way he just looked at his mom. "My dad didn't kill those women. He didn't!" I know the kid always defended his dad, but this time . . . something in his insistence . . .

Kerry bends closer to him and speaks into his ear. I barely hear her words. "Don't make this harder than it has to be."

He shakes off her hand. "No. I don't understand. Why'd you go looking for him in the first place? He'd still be alive."

She grabs him by the shoulders and dips her chin, leaning closer and looking directly into his eyes. "I've already told them the truth, son. They don't believe me. I thought he was guilty, too, but I didn't know the truth. I didn't believe you, please forgive me for that. I didn't even believe your father until now."

He leans into her, wrapping his arms around her midsection, turning his face toward me. "Don't take my mom. She didn't do anything wrong. She just wanted to come tell me the truth."

"We'll get that all sorted out, Joey. I . . ." I start to say promise, but I know he won't believe me. Why would he?

"I have to go, son."

"No."

She gently pries his arms away. "Go to Pops. Now."

He pushes away and runs toward the cabin.

She watches him go.

I process their words. *Strange Murders* reinforced our belief that Lucas was guilty. He was tried and convicted by reality television. Worse yet, we didn't even look at other possible suspects. A monster has been on the loose all these years because of that damn show.

I listen, hopeful for some words of wisdom from Mama, but for the first time in years, she's completely silent. I step forward, handcuffs ready. "I'm going to do what I can to help you. I promise."

Her face twists in anger as she offers her hands. "I don't believe you."

My cell rings as I slap on the cuffs. It's Foley.

"She's in custody," I say. "I'm at her place, she came here looking for Joey—"

"Listen. We're at the scene in the woods. At Lucas's cabin, and Jones isn't here."

I glance at Kerry. "What do you mean?"

"She either lied, or he wasn't dead."

"The guns?"

"They're not here either."

My nerves sizzle on high alert as my gaze skims the woods and then back to the porch. Callan is no longer sitting in the rocker. I pocket my phone and pull my weapon. My throat tightens, anxiety zips through my veins, and the cabin door squeaks open. Joey steps forward, a gun pressed against the side of his skull.

A voice calls out, "Drop your weapon or I'll kill the kid."

I toss my gun down and hold out my hands.

Kerry cries out for her son.

Strange Murders: *"Return of the Hatchet Killer"*
(Currently in production)

Unedited interview with local tattoo artist, Pony Malloy: Everyone has something in mind when they come into my shop, and Yates was no different. He wanted a screaming eagle descending on its prey with open talons. It seemed to have a special meaning to him. After the bodies were found, people started speculating about it, saying that getting inked was part of his pre-killing ritual, or some bull crap like that. Like all people who get inked are bad people. All I got to say, is that since the Yates tat went viral, I've had requests to do the same one on teachers, waitresses, a couple attorneys, and a cop. Yeah, a cop. They all want the Hatchet Killer's tattoo. Does that mean they're all going to go out there and start a killing spree? Get real, people. Tattoos are art, and art is for everybody.

THIRTY-FIVE

Kerry Grey

"Joey," my voice is a dry whisper. How can this be happening? Wyatt was dead. I pushed him and he was dead . . . but now he's here and he has Joey.

This is my fault. I should have made sure he was dead.

"Walk forward. Both of you," Wyatt calls out.

My hands are cuffed in front of me. I beg Nash, "Slip me the keys."

"Don't be stupid. He's got a gun."

"He's got my son."

"Just do what he says and maybe Joey will have a chance."

Maybe Joey will have a chance. "Let Joey go. I'll do whatever you want, just let—"

"Walk!"

We walk, fear and rage building inside me with each step. My heartbeat reverberates in my head, and everything around me fades to a blur except Joey and the gun bouncing against his skull. "We're going to die," I say, my voice like dry dirt. "He's here to kill me. He has nothing to lose, he's already going to prison for life."

Nash seems strangely calm, stoic even. Each step is solid and calculated, his gaze unwavering. But I see something welling in him, anger or fear, I can't be sure. His nostrils are pulsating, his jaw tight, and his words forced as he yells, "The kid hasn't done anything wrong. Let him go."

"He was born wasn't he? That's what he did wrong. He should've never been born. She was in love with me until she got pregnant with Lucas's kid."

Another step, and another, and in the shadows behind Joey a dark lump takes shape. It's Pops, crumpled on the floor like a discarded rag doll.

Pops is dead. Joey is next. "Why are you doing this, Wyatt? Why?" But I already know. There's a hairline trigger that turns extreme love into extreme hate. In Wyatt, his hate was fueled by hurt and a sick mind, until he became consumed with the need to hurt back. And now he intends to strip me from everything I love, to see me suffer, before he kills me.

"I'm not doing this, Kerry. You've done this. This is your fault. I want you to remember that, you hear me? Your fault. It's your lies, your wicked ways." His voice is high-pitched, whiny, surreal, almost childlike. Shivers break over my body, sweat drips down my back as I watch the gun slide lower on Joey's head. It's almost in his eye now. Wyatt continues, "You lied to me. That day down by the track, you told me that you loved me and that we'd be together forever. You're a liar. All women lie. All of you!"

We're close now. Close enough that I hear faint whimpers coming from Joey. A wet spot appears on the front of his jeans and spreads down his leg as the gun slides up and down his temple.

Wyatt screams out his next words, "What's taking you so long? Get over here now!"

Nash clenches my shirt from behind. "Easy," he whispers. "No sudden moves."

We're a couple feet from the porch. I can see Joey trembling.

"Let him go," I say. "And I'll do anything you want. Anything."

"It's a little too late for that now. Maybe if you'd been nicer to me out there in the woods, but you're just like the rest of them."

I put my weight on the first step of the porch. The dry boards squeak. Instantly, Joey is pushed aside. I rush forward, ready to cover him with my body when Wyatt appears in the doorway, the gun pointed inches from my face. I grab his hand, gripping and pushing it away at the same time. The gun goes off and wood splinters overhead, my ears zip, my nose stings, my whole head feels shattered, but I don't let go. I strain against the cuffs, inching my fingers forward, until I'm gripping the gun's barrel. The hot metal melts my skin as I force the gun higher, kicking my feet, connecting with the bone on his shins. There's a gruesome gash on his head, his hair matted to his skull, and blood dried in jagged lines over his face, giving him a monster-like appearance. Fitting.

He's been injured and weakened, and that gives me the advantage. He stumbles backward, and we fall into the cabin. Another shot fires, another and another, hot brass pelts my face, and then nothing. My head echoes with screams, Joey's and mine, and the empty gun falls to the ground. I swing my cuffed hands toward his head, miss, and I take a backhand to the face. Blood spurts from my nose, seeps between my lips, drains down my throat. I topple against the table, he's on top of me, his hands on my throat, his face inches from mine. I squirm and thrash but he's too strong and I'm losing strength. Dots appear on the peripheral of my vision, and close in, all I see are his eyes, dark and crazed, and then out of nowhere, a sickening *thunk*.

Wyatt releases me and I fall to the ground, gasping, like sucking through a collapsed straw. I raise my head and see Wyatt in a heap on the floor, and Nash, both hands clenched around the handle of a heavy cast-iron skillet. He raises it over his head like an axe and brings it down on Wyatt's skull. Blood and grey matter spurt into the air, splattering the wall, the cabinets, me. Across the room, Joey stands paralyzed, his hands clenched as he watches the violence unfold. I rush to him and pull him away.

Strange Murders: *"Return of the Hatchet Killer"*
(Currently in production)

Unedited Interview with Brax Ryan, Founder of The Hatchet Club (continued): If you want my opinion, the real deterrent in this whole ordeal is the county sheriff's department. They've shut down access to the national forest entrances, forbidding us from entering and searching for Lucas, even though there's a bounty on his head. That's an outright infringement on our rights. They've even tried to pin some trumped-up charge of hit and run on me. Anything to keep me and my group from our efforts. What are they trying to hide? We already know they've been incompetent for four years—they should be grateful for any help, but no, they keep "doing their job," calling us the amateurs, and the killer stays on the loose. The citizens of Joy have every right to protect themselves. Especially when the local authorities continue to fail to do so.

THIRTY-SIX

Adam Nash

Late that night, I leave the hospital in a haze of emotional shock and start driving, passing by Wyatt's place, then turning down road after road, aimlessly wandering and staring through my speckled windshield until I eventually find myself on the right road to Joy.

My clothing is stiff with dried blood, Wyatt's blood. Overkill, someone had whispered, and blamed it on fear and adrenaline. Callan suffered head trauma but was still alive. He would remain in the hospital overnight for observation. I was told to go home and rest. But it'll be a while before I find any rest. My vehicle is silent, no radio, not even Mama's relentless voice, but my mind is overwhelmed. I can't purge the haunting sound of crunching bones. Nor can I unsee Kerry being loaded into the back of the police cruiser, her eyes vacant, her clothing blood-stained, her spirit destroyed. And Joey, at the last moment, as he rushes toward the cop car and falls to the ground, his hands stretched outward as he lets out a sound like a wounded rabbit, and at the end of the anguish, his chest heaves right before he screams at the top of his lungs, "I love you, Mama."

The memory of his words cut open my chest like . . . a hatchet . . . and echo in my mind, *I love you, Mama, I love you, Mama* . . . My collar rubs against my neck, and I realize that it's soaked through. I've been weeping for my own mother. Her words absent in my mind now. All this time I've tried to quiet her voice, drowning it with alcohol, and now . . . what I wouldn't give to hear a reassuring word or two from her.

I barely make it out of bed before noon Saturday. I'm bruised and sore and nauseous, but I should go to the hospital and check on McCulley or go to the department to see if there's been a development in Hendrick's case, or get caught up on parolee files, or . . . or anything halfway productive, but I end up driving toward The Gold Bar. I need to assuage my physical pain and loosen the tight feeling in my gut.

The Gold Bar is the only place in town to eat other than the café, and attracts a varied clientele: families grabbing a burger for lunch, businesspeople connecting and making deals, folks trying to double their weekly paycheck on video poker, as well as the usuals who line the bar, nursing their alcoholism.

The bartender looks up as I enter, as do the other folks, sliding their gazes my way one by one, before turning back to the corner mounted television. The media replays clips of recent happenings: the protest, Kerry's arrest, or a body being removed from the jail on a gurney. They don't know yet about the accident or Kerry's escape, Wyatt Jones's death at my hands, or that Kerry's been taken back into custody. They are a few steps behind the facts; seems I was a few steps behind the truth as well.

I seat myself. The waitress plops down rolled silverware and holds out a menu. I wave it off and order a burger and beer. Tidbits of a conversation between two guys at the end of the bar float my way. "At least they got that Yates woman. Hope she rots in prison this time." Their conversation mixes with other similar discussions from patrons, their voices coming to me loud and clear. The one absent voice: Mama's.

I keep my head down, my beer comes. And then another. Three beers and a burger later, I feel more relaxed and like I can take on the rest of the afternoon, but then the door swings open and Brax walks in, flanked by two of his buddies. My teeth clench, and my neck chords strain against my collar. I stand and storm his way.

His eyes go wide, and he turns back toward the door.

"Hey. Hold up!"

He stops, his back to me for a couple beats before he turns around with an amused smirk on his face. I'd like to swipe his lips right off his head. "You ran us off the road yesterday," I bite out.

"Not me."

"I saw you."

"You're harassing me because I organized the protests against the sheriff and his incompetent deputies. They're nothing but a bunch of bullies who wouldn't let us pursue a killer. Maybe if they'd been more open to our help, there wouldn't be another dead body."

Out of the corner of my eye, I see the bartender draw a pint, lean back, and chug. We have everyone's attention, a little afternoon floorshow. Even the video poker area has gone quiet.

I shift my stance. "You were in a black Suburban. I saw you right before you ran into us."

He looks to the bartender who shrugs like they share some sort of secret.

"You almost killed us," I repeat. "An officer was badly injured."

"I'm sorry to hear that, but it wasn't me. I don't even own a Suburban." There's a hint of tremor in his voice.

"No. Not you. You weren't driving. One of your friends was behind the wheel. Maybe one of these guys here."

"I don't like what you're implying. Do you have proof, or are you just slinging accusations around?"

Movement to the right catches my attention, and I see a guy emerge from the back room with a small handheld camera. He points it at my table and the ketchup smeared plate and empty beer mugs, then pans back to me. Another guy joins him. I feel my mouth drop open and clamp it closed.

Mama? Are you there, Mama? Look who's here. It's him!

"Sorry to keep you waiting, Mr. Steele," Brax says. "This gentleman is Kerry Grey's Parole Officer. Nash is the last name, isn't it?"

I swallow back the spit in my mouth and look at Mr. Steele, *Strange Murders'* long-time host, standing next to the photographer. How many years had Mama and I waited for a moment like this?

Brax seems confident now. "He's questioning me about an accident that happened yesterday. I know nothing about it. I was with these guys all day." He looks at his friends. "Isn't that right?" They nod. "But as long as I've run into you, I have a few questions of my own. And I'm sure Mr. Steele is interested in your answers."

Steele smiles my way as his photographer repositions his black lens directly at me, and Brax continues, "Did Kerry Yates tell you where Lucas is hiding? Is that why the sheriff and several heavily armed rangers took off in a chopper yesterday? And whose dead body was hauled out of the jail?"

The camera zooms in on me and the voice Mama and I have listened to all these years speaks, "Do you have any answers for us, Mr. Nash?"

I remember Amber's warning. Foley gave orders that no one on the force is to talk to the show people. A few unintelligible syllables dribble from my mouth before I clamp my lips tight, shake my head several times, toss a couple bills on the table, and walk away.

* * *

I drive off, circling back to the hospital, replaying the events at the bar and wishing I could get Mama's take on everything. *Did you hear that punk kid talk to me like that? In front of Wesley Steele? The Wesley Steele?*

I shut out everything from my brain, go on autopilot, as I enter the hospital's double doors. McCulley's in a neck brace, and being held for observation for a possible concussion, but other than that, he's fine. I expected Callan to be there, too, but he'd already been released. A good sign. One of the few.

I go back to the department and spend a couple hours off the clock writing reports on the accident and Kerry's arrest. The beer has made the work tolerable but the progress slow. I keep a steady pace though and avoid looking at the empty cell, which still emits a faint death odor. I'm anticipating the findings from Hendricks's death investigation, wondering if I'd made a mistake and should have listened to what he had to say. It might have been something important, or it might have been nothing at all. You just never know with a guy like Hendricks.

I name Brax in my accident report, but McCulley told me that he didn't see the driver or any of the occupants. There is a BOLO out on a black suburban with passenger side damage. My guess is that it's been dumped somewhere.

As I write the report on Wyatt's death, I wonder if I'll have a job tomorrow, or if my episode of overkill would get me fired, maybe even land me in legal trouble. I'm halfway through when Foley comes downstairs. He leans against my desk and says, "Didn't expect to see you here today."

I shut down my computer and turn off my desk lamp, ready to face whatever he's going to throw my way. I've screwed up once again. First with Miranda, then getting everything wrong about Kerry, and bludgeoning Wyatt Jones. No wonder Mama's nowhere to be found.

Foley takes the chair across from me and quietly clears his throat. "We got a full statement from Kerry this morning."

I rub at my neck and shoulders. *I'm sorry, Mama. I thought we were so close. Guess I had it all wrong, wrong, wrong . . .*

"We searched Jones's place." He takes a deep breath and fidgets. The chair squeaks under his weight. "You ever patch things up with your wife?"

"My wife?"

"Yeah. Amber said that you two had a fight. Did you make up?"

"No." I reach over and tap my phone and scroll through a few of my unanswered texts. "She's not even answering my texts. Been over four days now. We've had fights before, but nothing like this."

"Have you tried reaching out to her family?"

I sit back. "Why all the questions about Miranda?"

"Just answer me, Nash. Her friends haven't heard from her? Her family? No one?"

"She doesn't have much family. A mother and sister, that's about it. They're estranged. Haven't talked for years. I've talked to most of her friends, left some messages for the ones I can't reach, but so far . . ."

A sheen of sweat breaks over his face.

"You okay, Foley?"

He holds his phone down to my eye level and shows me a photo. "Do you recognize this?"

I take the phone and look closer. "It's my wife's purse. What—?"

"After Kerry's statement, we searched Wyatt's place. This was in the crawl space under the house. It has Miranda's ID in it."

My hand trembles, and he takes the phone back. "We're running tests now, but the initial blood typing shows a match between what's on this purse and the tissue remains in the woods."

I shake my head several times. "What are you saying? That Miranda is . . . she's . . .?"

He places his hand on my shoulder. "I'm sorry."

Strange Murders: *"Return of the Hatchet Killer"*
(Currently in production)

Interview with Dani White Elk: I've known both Kerry and Wyatt since we were kids. We used to play together right here, in these woods, and when we were teenagers, Kerry and I worked together at the café downtown. We were close at one point, but then we drifted apart after she started dating Lucas. Mostly because I didn't care for him, or the way he treated her. The night she was arrested, we were at The Gold Bar together, at a party, and she confided in me that she'd just found out that Lucas was having an affair with one of the Hatchet Killer's victims. I think at that point she believed he was the one who killed them. She was terrified. She planned to leave him that night, after the party, then . . . well, she was arrested. We didn't stay in contact while she was in prison. I was surprised when she showed up at my house the other morning, asking for my help. She was in bad shape and was going on about Wyatt being the Hatchet Killer. To be honest, I didn't know what to think. I was scared. I knew the police were looking for her. On the news they said that she was suspected in the murder of that woman they found in the woods . . . something about finding the murder weapon in Kerry's barn. Anyway, as soon as I got the chance, I called the police. They came out and arrested her right there in my house.

THIRTY-SEVEN

Adam Nash

I call Rachel on the way home and ask her to use the spare key and the back door. She's waiting for me in a darkened living room. "Oh, Adam, I'm sorry. I'm so sorry."

She pulls me close. I inhale her scent and take comfort in her body pressed against mine.

"I can't believe it," she whispers against me. "Just can't. How did they find out it was her?"

I shudder and let out a long sigh against her neck.

She pulls back a little and points to the coffee table where there's a bottle of bourbon and two partially filled highball glasses. "Sit, sit," she says, and I do. She perches next to me, fills a glass and offers it to me.

The liquid warms me, calms me, loosens me, and I start to break. "I thought . . . we had a fight and the last thing I did was scream at her. I told her if she was so damn unhappy then she ought to leave. And now . . . was that the last thing she remembered before he . . .? Oh no . . ."

"Shh. Shh." She rubs small circles on my back, then leans closer and kisses my neck up to my jaw. I turn, my lips finding hers. I moan and shift and push her into the cushion.

"Wait," she whispers. "Shouldn't we wait. This feels like . . . I don't know." She squirms out from underneath me. "I mean, Lucas Yates just killed your wife."

"Not Lucas." I whisper, reaching for her again. Why isn't she comforting me? "It was never Lucas. It was Wyatt. Just like we thought."

"I knew it." She places her hand on my chest and pushes me back. "Wyatt . . . he's . . ."

"He's dead."

Her eyes widen. She drops her arm.

"That's right," I say. "And Lucas, too. They're both dead."

Her expression changes. She stiffens. "They're both dead," she repeats. "So the reward money—"

"The reward money?" The room goes cold. I sit back and take in her smeared lipstick, mussed hair, and I see the look of disappointment on her face. So much for our shared passions. She's not interested in me. Never has been.

I should have listened to you, Mama. You're always right when it comes to women.

I take a long drink of bourbon and reach for the bottle. "How well do you know Brax?"

She shrugs.

I top off my drink. "You know anyone in his crowd who drives a dark SUV?"

She stands and pats down her hair. "A dark SUV . . . how would I know? Why?"

"I had a run-in with a dark SUV. It forced us off the road, about killed us all. A deputy's hospitalized."

"That's horrible. I'm glad you're okay."

I'd been thinking about the encounter and putting it together in my mind. It came to me earlier at the bar, when I saw that camera pointed at me. When Brax leaned out the window of the SUV, he'd had a camera in his hand. He was taking footage of the transport. He wasn't trying to run us off the road, but film Kerry being transported. The guy's an opportunist, and reward money, or selling paparazzi-like photos to the press, would turn an extra buck. "I saw him at The Gold Bar. He seemed tight with the *Strange Murders* people. Is he trying to sell them information? Or maybe to some other people in the press."

"I have no idea what Brax is doing. You'd have to ask him." She picks up her purse. "I should be going. I really have so much to . . . oh, and Marco called. He's coming home tonight. So . . . well, I'll be busy for a while. You understand, right?"

"Yeah, I get it." I stand and take the bottle and my glass and walk past her toward the stairs. "Show yourself out, okay."

As soon as she's gone, I climb the stairs, bypassing our bedroom and stumbling toward the narrow, rickety stairs that lead to the attic. I stare up at the door, locked since the night Miranda left. She hated the attic and resented the time I spent in there. Too much time. Not just in the attic, but on this case. Guilt surges through me.

I haven't gone in the attic since that night. Won't go in there tonight either. Not yet.

Soon though.

Strange Murders: *"Return of the Hatchet Killer"*
(Currently in production)

Final interview with Sheriff Foley, Lewis County Sheriff in charge of the Hatchet Killer investigation: We've pursued Lucas Yates for nearly five years, and I would have never expected this case to take the turn it did. When my team found partial remains of the latest victim, we were sure it was another killing spurred by Kerry Yate's being release from prison. And when a hatchet, with blood that matched the victim's blood type, was found on Kerry's property, we issued a warrant for her arrest. But she'd already fled her residence. We put everyone in the field searching for her: forest rangers, deputies, reserves . . . everyone. We didn't track her down, but we lucked out and got a 911 call from Dani White Elk, a former friend of hers. Kerry had shown up at her place. Dani did the right thing in calling us. We were able to apprehend Kerry at approximately 7:00 a.m. that morning. While in custody, she gave information that led to the body of Lucas Yates. A crime scene investigation and later ballistics reports confirm that Wyatt Jones shot and killed Lucas Yates. Mr. Jones was later killed during a hostage standoff, where he threatened a young boy. Our continued investigation efforts turned up evidence at Wyatt Jones's home that points to an unhealthy obsession with Kerry. I believe it was that obsession that motivated the original hatchet killings, perpetrated, as we now know, by Mr. Jones. We also found at his residence the purse and ID of our latest victim. We, as a department, mourn the fact that she has been identified as

Miranda Nash, *wife of our county parole officer, Mr. Adam Nash. I'm now fully convinced that Wyatt Jones planted the original evidence that led to the warrant for Lucas Yates and to Kerry's incarceration. Kerry has been cleared of all criminal charges and will receive exoneration pay from the state of Montana.*

THIRTY-EIGHT

Adam Nash

It's been three weeks since that horrible day at the cabin, but already the trees have changed from that light green, barely there foliage, to a thick, heavy laden green. Humidity hangs in the air, and my shirt sticks heavy on my back. Other things have changed over the past weeks, too. We had a memorial service for Miranda. Hundreds of folks attended, many who I didn't know, some who I haven't seen for years. I would have preferred a quieter goodbye, but in a way, Miranda and I said our good-byes a long time ago.

Amber was fired. The investigation found tetrahydrozoline hydrochloride in trace amounts of leftover soda still in his takeout cup. It's a vasoconstrictor, which means it restricts coronary circulation, not a good thing for Hendricks's already drug-damaged heart. It's also the main ingredient in Amber's eye drops. Investigators found several emptied eyedrop containers in the back-alley trash can with Amber's prints on them. She swore that she was framed, that someone took them from her desk drawer, but no one is buying her story. Surveillance cameras showed her delivering his food that evening. She claims that I checked the delivery before she gave it to him, but she couldn't come up with proof of that, and . . . well, all the evidence points her way. It didn't help that they had a previously established relationship and were known around town to have been heavy partiers.

I testified in Kerry's defense at her hearing, and the judge granted her release. Public opinion of her shifted when it was revealed that Lucas was innocent, and she'd been wrongly imprisoned. She's been exonerated and won't serve any more prison or parole time, but those four years without Joey . . . nothing could ever make up that.

Now, I'm here, on the edge of the Grey's property, waiting for her to return home. Me and half the town, plus the *Strange Murders* crew who hopes to immortalize her homecoming. They've stuck around the past few weeks, interviewing folks about Wyatt Jones, filming reenacted segments of the case, and capturing live footage of Kerry's hearing. The producer, a woman who reminds me a lot of Mama, approached me and asked for an interview. Apparently, the show people have changed their tune toward the sheriff's department since Brax has been implicated in the hit and run that injured Deputy McCulley. We'd found the Suburban in a used car lot down in Bozeman and tied it to the bartender. I was right, Brax and several members of the Hatchet Club had been selling photos to the press, not mainstream media so much, but to the chop and dice tabloid-like media outlets. He also fessed up to sending the "leg" to our office. He's one disturbed young man. Now, of course, all the media has jumped on the Kerry Yates bandwagon, even *Weird Stories Online*, my favorite gossip rag. Anyway, it was tempting to say "yes" to the producer. I'd always dreamed of being on *Strange Murders*, but in the end, I declined. I usually don't make those type of decisions without Mama's input, and I still haven't heard from her.

Like everything else in life, I didn't appreciate Mama enough when I had her. I'd been so lucky to hear her sound advice through all this, not to mention all the things she did for me as a boy. And what did I do? Tried to drown her out. *I'm sorry, Mama. Please come back.*

Silence.

And then an uptick in excitement amongst the crowd. Wesley has been spotted exiting a dark sedan and moving across the lawn to where the crew of *Strange Murders* is huddled. Yes, I called him Wesley, not Mr. Steele like everyone else. We're on a first name basis now. I've talked to him informally a couple of times leading up to today. Our last conversation was especially rememberable. He came to the department, and even downstairs to my office, to sit with me and express his condolences on the death of my wife. "Perhaps," he told me. "You can find some solace in the fact her killer is dead and will no longer rob innocent women of their lives."

"Yes," I said. "Yes, I could find some peace in that."

He nodded and we discussed the show he hosted, and the case, and all these years in search of the Hatchet Killer. It struck me, during our conversation, that we're a lot alike, Wesley and me. We're both men on a quest for truth. And justice.

Now even more excitement fills the air with a hot buzz as a Bronco is spotted coming down the road. Cameras swivel, reporters scramble from the news vans that line the road, and onlookers press forward. They drive by, and I catch a glimpse of Joey with his face buried in Kerry's shoulder. Her gaze slides my way, and her chin raises slightly in a manner which says, "I can't believe how far we've come in all this." Kerry and I have endured a lot together and developed a mutual respect.

Callan pulls the Bronco close to the cabin and parks. The crowd watches in anticipation as Kerry steps from the passenger side with Joey. Several folks run up to them, crowd in, and call out her name. Cameras click off a cacophony of photos—*ka-chick, ka-chick, ka-chick.*

There are high hopes of a comment or two, maybe even a

brief interview, but she barely glances at the cameras, or the crowd, leaving everyone hungry for more details, or perhaps a tad bit about her future plans. She gives them nothing. Instead, she simply walks into the cabin, hand in hand with Joey.

As for Kerry's plans, she confided in me the other day that she'll take her grandfather and son and relocate as soon as possible. Joy is no longer her home. Maybe it never really was.

I realize, as I turn to and watch the crowd dissipate, that I'm not sure it's mine either.

Strange Murders: *"Return of the Hatchet Killer"*
(Currently in Production)

This is Wesley Steele, your host for Strange Murders. *You've just seen a clip of actual footage of Kerry Yates return home after her recent exoneration. Behind us is the home where she grew up and now lives with her grandfather, Callan Grey, and her son. In just moments you will hear crucial updates and the final twist of this bizarre and unusual case. Stay tuned for the conclusion of Return of the Hatchet Killer.*

THIRTY-NINE

The next morning, I turn in my resignation. My work is done here. And I believe that Mama, if she were to talk to me again, would tell me that it's time to move on to bigger and better things. I miss Mama's voice. I miss the time when we spent our days together on the sofa of my childhood home, the two of us watching *Strange Murders*, ferreting clues, and spewing our own version of justice. And I especially long to hear her call me her armchair detective, just one more time.

It also made me think about Wyatt and his relationship with his own mother. Did he sometimes hear her voice? Is it what turned him into a killer? Maybe. I've come to believe that evil takes root whenever toxic nurture invades the soul, perverting the mind until reality becomes so tightly twisted, it snaps. That's what happened to Wyatt.

Maybe that's what happened to me.

But all that doesn't really matter anymore. I'm leaving Joy behind me forever. This house that Miranda loved so much, the one I always hated, has sold sight unseen to a nice young couple from California. "My dream home," the woman said over the phone. Then she giggled. "Big enough to start a family."

Good luck to them.

Now all that's left is packing and cleaning.

* * *

I unlock the attic for the first time in over a month, since Miranda last stepped foot in here really, and carry in cleaning supplies. Everything is the way I'd left it that night, and a mixture of excitement zips through me just being in here again, then anger as I look down at the broken pieces of glass on the floor. Mama's picture. My favorite one of her in her yellow polka dot dress and white hat. I cherished it. Miranda hated it. Envy, that's what it was. And that night, when she called Mama a bad name, and smashed this picture on the floor, well . . . I snapped. I had to make things right.

I pick up the frame, carefully clearing away the jagged shards into the trash can, and then I replace the glassless frame back on its shelf. Front and center. *Right where you belong, Mama.*

I look around the attic and I think to myself: This is where it all started. Where I became the man my mother has always wanted me to be. Her little man. The man my father never was. Mama had once said of Daddy that he was nothing but a womanizer. Most men are.

Very true. Like Lucas Yates, ah hell, like me before all this, and Daddy was a cheater, too.

At least until he met such an unfortunate death.

I used to get sad thinking about Daddy's death. But over the years, Mama has explained it to me as one of those necessary evils. She'd always say, *It had to be done, boy. One day you may have to do the same thing, just to make things right.*

She was right. As always.

I place the bucket of hot water on the floor and slowly pour in the bleach, careful not to splash on my clothing. Instantly my attic room smells like the municipal swimming pool. I slip pink rubber dish gloves over my hands, dip, scrub, dip, scrub . . . and think to myself how beautifully it had all come together.

Miranda's out of my hair and finally at peace. Wyatt's dead, and with several women already hacked by his hand, what's one more murder pinned on him?

Too bad about Amber. Then I correct myself. Amber was nothing more than a flirt, always flaunting herself. Trouble, just like Mama said. In fact, she'd probably say, *Good riddance, boy.* Yes, that's exactly what Mama would say. If she were talking, that is.

I realize that I really am much happier without those women in my life. And Rachel, too. She's back with Marco, not giving me as much as a friendly wave these days. She only wanted me for one thing: information. I can't blame her. I understand how that desire to find answers, solve a case, gain notoriety or, in her case, money, can influence our interactions with others. I forgive her. *She's very much like I remember you being at that age, Mama.* No response, but I *feel* as if Mama's must be happier now. She's the only woman in my life again. (She was never good at sharing.)

I almost regret Hendricks though. Almost. Hendricks saw my vehicle that night out in the woods, not Wyatt's, and I couldn't have it tied to the body they found, to Miranda's body, so . . . well, Amber's history with the man and her addiction to eye drops provided the opportunity to fix that. To make things right.

I take time to go back downstairs and empty my bucket, and refill it with fresh water and bleach. I dip and scrub for a while longer, my thoughts returning to another time so long ago when I helped Mama clean up after Daddy had died. So much blood then, so much now.

Mama always did say that it's important to clean up your own messes.

Dip, scrub, dip, scrub . . . I pull out my penlight and shine it into the crevices between the floorboards. *All clean.* And then I look up, my gaze landing on Mama's picture, and smile. Mama had taught me so many lessons over the years, how to become free of toxic people and how to take care of any problems that come my way. How to recognize clues, so very helpful. Each lesson was taught and learned right there in that small, dingy living room in front of the television. But perhaps the most important lesson I learned from Mama was that while solving a crime is a rush, nothing compares to getting away with murder.

That's right, my little armchair detective.

ACKNOWLEDGMENTS

Thank you to literary agent Jessica Faust, who championed this story. For nine years and ten books, I was fortunate to have you on my side. We had a good run.

To Dan Mayer, my editor at Seventh Street Books, you made this story so much better, and I can't thank you enough. Ditto to all the publishing team at Start Publishing, in particular Marianna Vertullo, Ashley Calvano, and copyeditor, Patrick Smith. And thank you to publicist Wiley Saichek, who is skilled in bringing authors and readers together.

A big thank you to Sandra Haven-Herner, freelance editor and mentor, for your patience and guidance. This one was complex, but you managed to pull me out of plot holes and keep me on track. Thanks, my friend.

Thank you to the following professionals who generously offered their time to help me with the facts of this story: Kevin Kirby, MD, thank you for answering all my hypothermia questions. I'm grateful for your expertise. Thank you to D.P. Lyle, MD who answered my autopsy questions and knew everything there is to know about poisoning my character. And a huge shout out to retired Probation Officer Sharon Moseson, who graciously took time to fill me in on the nuances of probation and parole work.

And lastly, thanks to all my writer friends, especially my Wednesday Writer's Group. Even though I've missed a ton of

Wednesdays, I always feel your support. Mom and Dad and Sibs: you're the best family ever. And biggest hugs of all to my husband and our children. God has blessed me.